DEMCO

ALIBIS AND LIES

Other books by Ilsa Mayr:

The *Cybil Quindt Mystery* series:

Alibi for a Cold Winter's Night
Banker's Alibi
A Timely Alibi

Maelstrom
Serenade
Summer Flames
Portrait of Eliza
Gift of Fortune
Dance of Life

ALIBIS AND LIES

•

Ilsa Mayr

AVALON BOOKS
NEW YORK

Published by Thomas Bouregy & Co., Inc.
160 Madison Avenue, New York, NY 10016

Library of Congress Cataloging-in-Publication Data

Mayr, Ilsa.
    Alibis and lies / Ilsa Mayr.
        p. cm.
    ISBN 978-0-8034-7759-9 (hardcover : acid-free paper)
    1. Women private investigators—Fiction.   2. Missing
persons—Investigation—Fiction.   3. Adopted children—
Fiction.   4. Inheritance and succession—Fiction.
5. Extortion—Fiction.   I. Title.
    PS3613.A97A8 2010
    813'.6—dc22
                                                      2009045794

PRINTED IN THE UNITED STATES OF AMERICA
ON ACID-FREE PAPER
BY HADDON CRAFTSMEN, BLOOMSBURG, PENNSYLVANIA

ALIBIS AND LIES

Chapter One

"Who wants to see me?" I asked, pressing the receiver a little closer to my ear.

Lynn, our Vietnamese receptionist and office manager, had a good command of the English language, but occasionally had trouble pronouncing proper names. I told her I'd come down to the reception desk. She slammed down the receiver. Wincing, I wondered with whom she was angrier: me or herself.

Halfway down the curving stairs, I slowed down so that I could study the woman standing in front of the wooden gate that separated Lynn's desk from the waiting area. Irritation flared through me. The woman looked to be somewhere in her seventies, yet Lynn hadn't invited her to step past the gate where two comfortable chairs were grouped around a coffee table. I rushed down the rest of the stairs. Hearing me approach, the woman turned toward me.

"I'm Cybil Quindt, apprentice investigator with the Keller Agency. Can I help you?"

"Oh, I hope so. I'm Rose MacNiall."

She offered me her leather-gloved hand, which I shook. I'd heard that name before, but at the moment couldn't think in what context. "Why don't we go into the conference room?" I suggested, pointing toward the door to the right of the front entrance.

Ignoring Lynn's hissed breath, I led Mrs. MacNiall to the conference room and shut the door firmly behind me. This would irritate Lynn, who was the nosiest person I knew. She resented being left out of anything. Somehow she'd make me suffer for shutting the door, but I didn't care.

Uncle Barney, who owns the Keller Agency, was the only one who escaped Lynn's wrath because I strongly suspected that they had a history together. I also suspected that she was more than a little in love with him. At work he treated her with the old-fashioned courtesy of a bygone era. How he treated her outside the office, or even if he had occasion to meet her after business hours, I didn't know. Uncle Barney was extremely discreet and reticent about his private life.

Mrs. MacNiall placed her handbag on the conference table in front of her before she sat down. The bag looked just like the kind seen dangling from Queen Elizabeth's arm ever since she'd assumed the British throne.

"Would you like to take off your cape?" I asked, suspecting that the green loden garment would be lined and very warm. The conference room was heated.

She made a dismissing gesture with her hand, but she did loosen the clasp on the cape, revealing a strand of singularly beautiful pearls. They matched the pearls in her earrings.

"Let's get down to business," she said.

She touched the black felt hat she wore as if to make sure it sat straight on her gray-streaked hair. She hadn't let her hairdresser dye it apricot or bluish white or any of the odd colors often seen on elderly ladies. I liked that.

I sat down across from her and pulled the yellow legal pad closer. The Bic pen on it was clicked and ready for use. When Mrs. MacNiall kept silent—apparently struggling with what she wanted to say—I asked again, as softly and nonthreateningly as I could, "How can I help you?"

"It's a difficult problem. Complicated . . ." Her voice trailed off. Then she leaned toward me. "This is confidential, is it not?"

"Absolutely. And most problems discussed in this office are complicated. Can you tell me in a sentence or two what it is that brought you to this agency? What you want us to do?"

"Find my granddaughter."

She surprised me. Most people hemmed and hawed, repeated themselves and never managed to state their wishes so clearly without being guided through a series of leading questions.

So, this was going to be a missing persons case. They could be astonishingly simple or devilishly difficult.

"What is your granddaughter's name?" I asked, prepared to write it down.

"I'm not sure. When she was born, my daughter told the midwife that her name was Chelsea. Liza selected that name. We certainly wouldn't have."

Her nose twitched as if she wanted to sniff derisively, but restrained herself.

"Who is we?"

"The rest of the family. We would have picked a name that had been in the family for generations, a biblical name like Anne or Elizabeth or Mary."

It was on the tip of my tongue to point out that Rose wasn't exactly a biblical name, but stopped myself.

"And Chelsea's last name?"

Mrs. MacNiall shrugged. She concentrated on pulling off her leather gloves, fingertip by fingertip. They seemed a little tight and this procedure took some time. I wondered if she used this tactic to give her time to think.

"I have no idea who the father of the baby is. My daughter refused to say."

When she saw my expression, she said, "Liza chose a lifestyle she was sure the family would disapprove of. Bohemian or hippy or whatever it was called."

Bohemian or hippy? The first suggested the fifties and the second the sixties and seventies.

"When was the last time you saw your daughter and granddaughter?"

"Let me think. Liza I saw a week ago at my husband's funeral, but before that we saw each other rarely though we spoke on the phone occasionally. And my granddaughter I've never laid eyes on."

Although Uncle Barney had drummed it into me that we never showed surprise at anything a client said, I knew my pen came to an abrupt stop. She had never seen her granddaughter? Pulling myself together, I quickly offered my condolences. Now I remembered where I'd come across the MacNiall name. The newspaper obituary had been detailed.

"How old was your daughter the last time you saw her before the funeral?"

"Liza was twenty-one. She came into part of her trust fund. I saw her at our lawyer's office. I'll see her there again when my husband's will is read."

"How old was Liza when Chelsea was born?"

"Seventeen which is how old Chelsea is now."

A teenage mother. "Did she keep the baby?"

"Heavens, no. Oh, she had some romantic notion that she could take care of the baby, but that was ridiculous. She couldn't even take care of herself."

"And the baby's father? You must have some idea. A boy she was seeing—"

"Liza stubbornly refused to tell us his name. I'd always assumed he was married."

Not an unreasonable assumption, I thought. "Was the baby given up for adoption?"

"Yes."

"Open adoption?"

Mrs. MacNiall stared at me. Finally she said, "I don't think that was an option back then."

"So Liza doesn't know who adopted her baby?"

"No."

I put down my pen and looked at her. "Do you know?"

She shook her head. "If I did, I'd hardly come to ask for your help and air out our dirty linen in your office."

It seemed that in some segments of society, an illegitimate child was still a disgrace. Briefly, anger flared in me. I had lost a child. I bit down hard on my lower lip to control the anger and the pain. Taking a breath, I said, "Let me summarize: Seventeen years ago your daughter Liza gave birth to a baby whom she called Chelsea. The baby was given up for adoption. You want the agency to find your granddaughter. Is that right?"

"Yes. Can you do it?"

I hesitated. "It'll be difficult. What else can you tell me?"

She shrugged.

"What hospital was your granddaughter born in?"

"She was born at home."

"Wasn't that unusual back then?"

Mrs. MacNiall drew herself up defensively. "Not at all. My daughter was born at home. All the better families in town had home births."

That was news to me, but then I didn't belong to one of the *better* families—at least not how Mrs. MacNiall probably defined them.

"Was a doctor there?"

"Eventually."

"His name?"

"Dr. Ralph Gideon. He was recommended by a family friend."

"Does he still practice?"

"I have no idea."

"What was the midwife's name?" I asked.

"Shirley something. Dwain or Dwight or Dwyer."

"Is she still in business?"

"I doubt it. She was already elderly seventeen years ago."

She avoided eye contact, and I wondered what she was holding back about the midwife. "What agency did you use to handle the adoption?"

"No agency."

It was on the tip of my tongue to ask if they'd left the baby on the steps of a church, but restrained myself. As I looked at her stern, thin-lipped face, I thought she might have been quite capable of doing just that.

"Who arranged the adoption?"

"The midwife."

"For a fee?"

"Of course, for a fee. Young woman, nothing in this life is free."

With the likes of Mrs. MacNiall, that was undoubtedly true. This wasn't a charitable thought, but being referred to as "young woman" in that tone irritated me.

"And speaking of fees, how much is this going to cost me?" she demanded. Her voice held a belligerent edge.

I wanted to tell her that our fee would be far less than the cost of the diamond-encrusted ruby on her right hand or the vulgarly large diamond engagement ring on her left, but merely handed her the agency brochure.

After putting on a pair of glasses suspended from a gold chain around her neck, she read the brochure carefully. She obviously wasn't the type to sign anything without studying it thoroughly.

"I see that you have two options. A flat fee or billable hours. You think it will take some time to find my grand-daughter?"

"With as little as we have to go on, yes," I answered truthfully.

She gave me a long look over the top of her glasses. "Then I'd be better off with the flat-fee option."

"Probably."

"Still, I don't want this investigation to drag on forever."

"Neither does the agency." Did she think we had no other clients? Or that dealing with her was such a pleasure that we were loath to give it up?

"Can you give me an exact amount?"

"Yes." I pointed to a sum in the column listing flat fees. "You can give us a ten percent deposit, and we'll take it from there."

Mrs. MacNiall studied the column of figures. "Very well, but I'll expect a weekly report."

"Biweekly," I said just because I didn't feel like being ordered around by this woman every week. Twice a month was more than enough.

She pulled a checkbook from her handbag and wrote a check.

"Lynn will give you a receipt and some forms to fill out. Routine information we need before we can get started." I pressed a button on the phone sitting on the conference table.

Moments later, a knock on the door told me Lynn was there with the necessary papers. Nothing propelled her into action faster than the prospect of a fee. She waited while our client filled out the forms.

Both of us accompanied Mrs. MacNiall to the door. Outside, a chauffeur leaned against a black Lincoln. When he saw Mrs. MacNiall, he jumped to attention and opened the back door for her.

Watching the elegant car drive away, Lynn said, "We could have charged her more." She looked at me accusingly.

"We don't operate like that. We stick to the listed fees."

"Except when we do cases for nothing. All that pro . . . whatever that word is."

"Pro bono."

"Yes, that one. Which *you* do a lot off," she said before flouncing to her desk.

I ignored her and took the forms to my upstairs office to study them.

Chelsea's mother was the obvious one to be interviewed first. She was most likely to remember the name of the midwife. Mrs. MacNiall had written her daughter's name as Liza MacNiall Miller Scott, listed the address in an apartment building near downtown, and Liza's profession as receptionist in a medical clinic near Mercy Hospital. That surprised me. An apartment in a low-rent district and a job that didn't pay a lot for the daughter of one of the richest families in town? Unexpected and unusual, to say the least.

I called the clinic. They closed at five.

Since Luke, my estranged physician husband, occasionally volunteered at this clinic, I had been there once or twice. It was a large facility and my chances of spotting Liza—of whom I had only the fuzzy description given by her mother—were slim to none. Instead I drove to her apartment building and parked across the street. I had a clear view of the parking lot as well as the front entrance.

The two-story house had been divided into two flats per floor plus an attic apartment. From the name tags next to the doorbells, I guessed that Liza lived on the top floor. I went back to my Volvo to wait.

As I'd been primarily watching the parking lot, I almost missed the woman who got off the city bus a block away. I always advocated public transportation but could only rarely use it due to the nature of my job, which often demanded instant mobility. I had automatically assumed that Liza would arrive home in a car. Mentally I kicked myself.

I compared the woman walking toward the house with her mother's description: thirty-four, with short, dark-blond hair—which was frosted—slender, and about five foot six. It fit.

I timed my arrival at the front entrance to coincide with hers. "Mrs. Liza Scott?"

"I'm Liza MacNiall. I've taken my maiden name back,"

she said, looking at me with suspicious eyes. "And I don't need any magazines or whatever you're selling."

"I'm not selling anything."

"Then what do you want?"

She unlocked the front door and stepped inside. Quickly, I placed my boot-clad foot on the doorstep to keep her from closing the door in my face.

"Your mother hired me to find Chelsea."

"What?" Liza whirled around to face me. "She did what?"

"Hired me to find your daughter." I noticed that angry red blotches broke out on her face.

"I don't believe this. I don't . . ." Her voice petered out. She shook her head. Then she turned toward the stairs. "You better come on up. I don't want to discuss this where everyone can hear it."

I followed her. The flight of steps to the attic was exceedingly steep. Falling down these stairs could be fatal. A shiver put goose bumps on my arms as I recalled my first case where such a fall had occurred.

By the time we reached the top, I was a little out of breath, reminding me that I hadn't swum as many laps recently as I ought to have. I promised myself to do better.

I followed her inside. The attic consisted of one large room with a small walled-in area in a corner, which I assumed was the bathroom. Liza bent down to pick up a towel and a pair of white panties off the floor. She tossed them onto the unmade bed.

"I didn't get a day off last week so the place is a mess.

The clinic's open seven days a week, so if someone doesn't show up one of us loses her day off. We get paid time-and-a-half, so it's not that bad, but still." She took off her coat and tossed it on the bed as well.

I wondered where she put all the stuff on the bed when she wanted to sleep. She swept a pile of newspapers from the couch and pointed to it.

"Have a seat." She dropped into a rocking chair, bent down to unlace her white nurse-type shoes and, with a sigh, removed them. "I'm not a nurse so I don't know why they make me wear these butt-ugly shoes." She looked at my boots. "I like those. Enough of a heel to look elegant but not so high as to be dangerous on ice. Where'd you buy them?"

"In Chicago at an after-Christmas sale."

"Don't you just love a good sale?"

"Doesn't every woman?"

"Not my mom. You've never met a woman who hates shopping more than she does. Orders everything by phone. Where's the fun in that?"

I shrugged, hoping my face expressed a complete lack of comprehension when, in truth, shopping was not my favorite pastime either.

"So, my mother hired you to find my daughter. And you're a . . . not a cop . . . a private cop?"

"Yes." I handed her my card.

Liza studied it. "Mmm. For Mother to actually spend money to hire someone is so out of character. I wonder what she's up to." She put the card down and took a cigarette from a pack on the end table and lit it with a match. "I'd ask if you minded me smoking but this is my apartment, and it's been a long and lousy day."

I watched her inhale deeply and with obvious pleasure. I stopped myself from telling her how bad that smoke was for her lungs, because she was a health professional and doubtlessly knew all the dangers better than I.

"Did my mother say why she wanted to find her granddaughter?"

I shook my head. "Maybe now that she's getting on in years she wants to see her. Maybe—" Liza's burst of laughter stopped me.

"I see that you don't know my mother. There isn't a single soft or sentimental bone in her body. She's the most coldly calculating woman you'll ever meet. Next to my grandmother who, to everyone's relief and probably to St. Peter's regret, was called to a better place. Come to think of it, St. Peter probably sent her south." She smiled, then growing serious, she asked, "Did you ask why Mom wants to find my girl?"

"No. We don't ask that question unless we suspect that the client intends to use what we discover to harm someone."

"And my mother struck you as harmless? A proper lady?"

"Yes," I said, thinking of the hat, the gloves, and the handbag. All that jewelry was perhaps a little vulgar. It would be interesting to get my grandmother's take on Rose.

Maxi was uncannily right in reading people. I bet she would consider wearing all that jewelry in daylight as a bit gauche.

Liza blew a couple of smoke rings before she spoke. "She wasn't always the grand dame of Westport, the wife and now widow of the former mayor and leading citizen of our fair city. Her maiden name was Rozalia Mae Zwick. And the Zwick was short for a name that had lots more consonants in it and ended in ski." Liza laughed sarcastically. "Rozalia Mae definitely came from the wrong side of the tracks."

Westport had a sizable Polish population, and hearing it disparaged surprised me. I'd thought we were more tolerant than that, even proud of our ethnic diversity. Didn't the whole city celebrate Dyngus Day with a huge consumption of Polish sausages?

Maybe my grandmother was right. Maxi claimed that I saw the world through a veil of idealism. Affectionately, she always added that this was not a bad thing, but a sign of optimism. Of a positive outlook. Of course, it could also be a sign of naiveté. If so, I had to guard against it, especially on the job. All the authors of hard-boiled PI novels would blanch at the thought of a gentle, maybe even wimpy, investigator. Mickey Spillane would call me a sappy dame.

"Rozalia Mae was ambitious and ruthless," Liza continued. "She met my father, and he was putty in her clever hands."

I'd always wondered how men became putty in a woman's hands. Luke, my estranged husband, never had. "How did she manage that?"

"You said the operative word: *manage.* My mother is very astute in assessing people's needs and weaknesses and then manipulating them. My dad's upbringing had been privileged and protected. He was shy and no match for her. Rozalia Mae got pregnant right away and after she produced an heir, she was in. Not that she was ever completely accepted, but my mother isn't the sensitive type. And then there was all that lovely money."

Although my relationship with my beautiful, often-married mother wasn't ideal, I hoped it would never sink to this acrimonious level.

"Rozalia Mae had everything: a husband from a fine family and wealth. What else could a girl from the wrong side of town want?"

Then, broodingly, she answered her own question.

"Maybe a daughter who didn't disgrace the family by having an illegitimate baby at age seventeen."

"Tell me about the baby."

"You wouldn't understand."

"Try me," I said.

"You have any kids?"

"I had a little boy. He . . . died."

"I'm sorry. Maybe you will understand." Savagely she ground what was left of her cigarette into the bottom of a glass ashtray. "You see, I wanted that baby. I was in love with her father. He couldn't marry me, but that didn't mean I didn't want his child."

"Why couldn't he marry you?"

She shook her head. "That doesn't matter. I made a deal

with my mother. If I stayed in the house for the last five months of my pregnancy, she'd let me keep the baby. I believed her. What a fool I was."

"What happened?"

"My mother convinced me that it would be better to have the baby at home. I did. A little girl. I called her Chelsea."

"You told the midwife that."

"Yeah." She paused. "They gave me something for the pain, so some of it is a little fuzzy. But I did get to hold the baby for a minute. I had been in labor for sixteen hours, and I was exhausted. I'd nod off for a moment between contractions. I think I heard babies cry."

"Babies? As in more than one?"

"Yeah, I think so. I know that sounds crazy . . ." Her voice trailed off. Liza pressed her hands against her temples. "I had a twin sister. She died a few hours after she was born. Don't twins run in families?"

I nodded.

"Sometimes I still dream of babies crying. Isn't it crazy how the mind won't let go of some things? Anyway, when I woke up, the baby I'd held briefly was gone. All traces of her had been removed. If it hadn't been for how my body felt, I'd never have known that I'd given birth."

I stared at Liza, too stunned to speak. The enormity of what was done to Liza by her mother and grandmother was staggering. Not only had they taken Liza's daughter, they'd lied about the other baby. There was probably only one reason for the lie. The other baby hadn't survived. But why was Rose still lying about it now? Finally, to break the long silence, I asked, "What did you do?"

"I screamed. I hammered on the locked door of my room until I started to hemorrhage and fainted. They kept me sedated for several days. When I was well enough to get up, I knew it was too late to find my baby . . . babies." She paused to rub her forehead. "I stuck around until I turned eighteen. Then I took the jewelry my great-grandmother left me and lit out for Chicago."

"You came back when you became eligible for your trust fund."

"Yeah. Except the wording of the fund was odd. I can only get a certain amount each month. Not the lump sum. That's why I live in this dump on a pitiful salary. And don't even suggest that I could live in the family mansion. I'd rather take a daily beating."

"Have you tried breaking this stipulation?"

"I never had the money to hire a first-rate lawyer. Not one good enough to fight my mother's army of attorneys."

"When and why did you move back to Westport?"

"A few years ago. And why? Because it's cheaper to live here than in Chicago."

That was true enough but I doubted it was the only reason. "Do you remember the midwife's name?"

"Yes. Shirley Dwyer. She was nice and caring."

"And the doctor's name?"

"I'm not sure. It wasn't our family doctor."

When I looked surprised, she laughed mirthlessly.

"You don't think my mother wanted anyone in her circle

to know her seventeen-year-old daughter was pregnant. She kept me a virtual prisoner in her house for the last five months of my pregnancy. I'm sure the midwife and the doctor were sworn to secrecy and well paid for their silence."

"Could it have been Dr. Ralph Gideon?"

"Gideon? That sounds vaguely familiar, but I couldn't swear to it."

"Is there anything else you remember that would help me find your daughters?"

Liza shook her head.

"At some point I may have to know the name of the father."

Liza shook her head. "Only if it's absolutely necessary."

"Does your mother know who he is?"

"I don't see how she could. I never told anyone. Promise me one thing?"

"If I can."

"Let me know first when you find my babies. Before you tell my mother."

"That would be unethical. She's our client."

"Then please promise to call me right after you tell her. And find out why she wants to locate them. I don't trust her. I have to protect them."

I looked into her eyes and saw that she was genuinely afraid. *What had I done by accepting this case?*

Uncle Barney. I had to talk to him immediately.

Chapter Two

I burst into the agency with unseemly haste. "Uncle Barney. I need to speak with Uncle Barney," I said, thoroughly out of breath.

"He's still down in Indianapolis," Lynn said. "Won't be back until tomorrow."

I muttered a mild swear word which earned me a censorious look. "I guess I can try his cell phone this evening."

"No! He's meeting with the state senator. A very important man. You cannot bother your uncle."

Watch me. Out loud I said nothing but headed upstairs to my office. Long ago I had learned not to get into an argument with Lynn. She relished a good shouting match. I didn't.

Sitting at my desk, I studied the notes I had taken in the meetings with the MacNiall women. I checked the

Westport phone book for the names of the nurse and the doctor. Nothing. Uncle Barney had taught me to start with Westport and then work my way outward.

I'd start with the southern part of the county. I grabbed the Minton directory. I'd always suspected that Minton was originally called Mint Town because the farms around the little village grew acres and acres of mint. During the summer the whole area smelled like chewing gum or mouthwash. I couldn't believe my eyes when I found Shirley Dwyer's name. Using the reverse directory, I found her address on Route 3.

Praying that my luck would hold, I searched for Dr. Ralph Gideon. Him I didn't find within a fifty mile radius of Westport. Before I wasted a whole lot of time, I needed to be sure that he wasn't listed in the obituary index. He wasn't, at least not in our immediate vicinity. Of course, the good doctor could have retired to the sunnier climes of Florida or the Southwest. Or he could be living with one of his children. If he had any.

Working in the same field, Shirley might know him or of him. Grabbing my coat and scarf, I headed out.

"Where are you going?" Lynn asked.

"Looking for a witness in the MacNiall case."

"Oh."

At the door I almost collided with Maxi.

"Oma!" I said and hugged her. "Did you come to see me?"

"Yes. I came to take you for coffee."

Maxi adhered to the continental custom of having afternoon coffee between three and four. In her younger years, she'd served delicious homemade pastries with coffee on her farm, but now only did it on special occasions. As I didn't need the extra calories, I didn't mind.

Starbucks had finally penetrated the Midwest market, so we always went there. Maxi ordered a latte and I a plain black coffee. Both of us virtuously avoided looking at the pastries in the display case.

"So, what's up?" I asked when we were seated at a small table by the window.

"Does something have to be up for me to see my favorite granddaughter?"

"I'm your only granddaughter," I reminded her with a smile.

"I still don't understand that with six children of my own, I ended up with only one granddaughter." She shook her head. "But since she is such a special woman, I guess I shouldn't complain." She patted my hand lovingly. "So, what are you working on?"

"You know I can't tell you specifics, but are you by any chance familiar with the MacNiall family?"

"Of course. Isn't everyone?"

I looked at her, startled. "I'm not."

Maxi thought for a moment, and then she nodded. "Of course. You were away at school. You missed the drama and the tragedy." She stared at the far wall.

"Are you going to keep the drama and the tragedy to yourself?"

"No, no." She took a breath before she started. "The

MacNialls had two children. The boy, Andrew, was two years older than Liza. He died under mysterious circumstances."

"What was mysterious? Cause of death?"

"Officially the cause of death was listed as heart failure."

I groaned in disbelief. "Ultimately, aren't all deaths due to heart failure? I mean, the heart stops pumping, doesn't it?"

Maxi shrugged. "There were plenty of rumors about alcohol and drugs but nothing was ever made public. When a young person dies, it's not unusual that such rumors circulate. Except I have it on good authority from a reliable source that amphetamines were involved. In large doses. You have to remember that there was a time when some doctors handed them out as if they were candy."

"I've heard that."

"By the time the police arrived and the ambulance had rushed Andrew to the hospital, there was no evidence of any drugs in the house."

"Just how hard can it be to flush a bunch of pills down the toilet or the garbage disposal," I said.

"Exactly."

"Did Andrew survive?"

"Tragically, no. His father never got over it. And Rose? Well, she's made of sterner stuff, but the boy was the apple of her eye. She must have suffered the pangs of hell, losing her boy."

"She did," I said softly.

Maxi placed her hand on mine. "I'm sorry I brought up dark memories for you."

"We can't always avoid talking about Ryan or death," I said. The small smile I attempted failed. I brooded for a while about my little boy before I spoke again. "What about Liza? Where was she during all this?"

"Largely ignored by her parents. Oh, they hired someone to look after her, but that's hardly the same thing. It's not surprising that she looked for affection elsewhere and got pregnant."

A line from a popular song popped into my head, a line about looking for love in all the wrong places. Poor Liza. What a price she paid for that love. We sipped our coffee, lost in our thoughts. Finally I roused myself. "Wouldn't you think that most families after losing a son would welcome grandchildren?"

"Most well-adjusted families would."

"And the MacNialls weren't the prototype for the all-American family?"

"More likely the prototype for the dysfunctional American family."

I waited for Maxi to elaborate.

"There was old Mrs. MacNiall. Patricia MacNiall, a real termagant."

"Termagant?" I asked with a smile. "The only other time I heard this word was in a lit class when we were reading an English comedy of manners."

"Trust me. It described James's mother to a tee."

"James being Rose's husband?"

"Yes. The poor man was like a ping pong ball between his wife and his mother, two strong women, for neither of whom he was a match."

Maxi was one of the few people who still scrupulously used *who* and *whom* correctly and insisted that all her children and grandchildren did the same.

"It must have been pretty awful for him, but I'm not sure it was all that awful for the women. I think they rather enjoyed their skirmishes," she said.

"Some people seem to thrive on strife. I've never understood that. Arguments, especially with people I care about, give me a stomachache."

"Like when you argue with Luke?"

"Yes. And with Mom. Good thing you and I don't argue. That would give me the worst stomachache of all."

"What specifically do you and Elizabeth argue about?"

"Unimportant, dumb things. How I dress. How I don't wear enough makeup. How my job is unsuitable. The last is also a major contention between Luke and me."

"The last objection I can sympathize with."

"Oma! Not you too."

"Only because your job can put you in danger. And it has. You can't deny that."

Unfortunately, I couldn't. I'd been knocked out, dumped into a lake, and shot at. "But it happens only rarely."

"Is that supposed to put our minds at ease?" Maxi asked, her tone ironic.

I ignored her statement. "Most of the time I search databases or ask people questions and write reports. Perfectly harmless tasks. I'm not a danger junkie, so stop worrying. Anyway, tell me about old Mrs. MacNiall."

"Well, she came from a wealthy family, which didn't help Rose."

"How did they make their money?" I asked.

"Patricia's grandfather invented something. I don't remember exactly what, but something that improved farm wagons, and since this was primarily farm and orchard country, he made a lot of money. And as people usually did back then, they married into their own socioeconomic class. Money begot money."

"Rose was the exception to that."

Maxi nodded.

"Couldn't have been easy for her."

"No, but she was tough, thick-skinned, and a quick study. I knew her from church. After a year or so among the Mac-Nialls, I hardly recognized her. The gregarious, lively girl had turned into a prim and proper lady, at least outwardly."

"I wonder how her husband felt about that. Maybe what had attracted him to Rose was exactly the thing she changed."

"How perceptive of you, Schatzi. I'm sure that's exactly what happened. I didn't travel in their circles, but James was on the library board, and though he was never the life of the party, after his marriage he grew even more . . . I don't know what to call it."

"Disillusioned? Disappointed?"

Maxi considered this. "Maybe, but I think the word *melancholy* is a better description."

"Not exactly a happy household for Liza to grow up in," I said.

"Well, you didn't exactly grow up in a settled, harmonious home either, not with Elizabeth getting married every time I turned around," Maxi said.

With a pang I realized just how much my grandmother minded my mother's divorces and marriages. Did she feel she had somehow failed to raise her daughter properly? How could she doubt herself? I couldn't think of a better mother than Maxi. Then I remembered something I'd always meant to ask her. "Oma, if my dad hadn't been killed in that accident, do you think Mom would have stayed married to him?"

"Isn't it pretty to think so."

"Quoting Hemingway? That line, it's the last one in *The Sun Also Rises*, isn't it? It always makes me want to cry." And it told me that Maxi had doubts about my parents' marriage lasting. A happy forever after for them had been a fantasy of mine for as long as I could remember. It made me sad to see it crumble into nothingness.

Maxi, being the observant, wise woman that she was, said, "I could be wrong. Your father was the first and the best of the men my daughter married. If anyone could make her happy for any length of time, it would have been him."

In silence we finished our coffee.

"I need to get back to work," I said. More specifically, try to locate Shirley Dwyer.

"And I need to stop by church to check the sign-up

sheet. The fish fry's on Friday. We appreciate all the business we can get. Hint, hint."

"I'll be there shortly after five. Save three servings, please."

We put our coats and gloves on, wrapped ourselves in our scarves, walked out together, hugged, and went our separate ways.

Route 3 snaked through the southwestern part of the county. Though the road was clear and dry, the fields were still covered by snow. Winter hung on long and grimly in northern Indiana.

Minton consisted of a dozen houses along the highway with a couple of parallel side streets completing the village. I passed a gas station, a white-pillared church, and a firehouse which I was sure would be manned by volunteers. The redbrick school house had been converted into the town hall. The children, I assumed, were bused to Westport schools.

Shirley Dwyer lived south of the village in a good-sized brick ranch house. A new SUV and a motorcycle were parked in the driveway. The SUV had a handicapped sticker on the rear window. I parked behind the Harley-Davidson.

Even through the closed door I could hear the television program and Dr. Phil preaching the riot act to some unlucky soul.

I had to ring the doorbell twice before the volume was turned down and the front door opened. The man facing me did not look happy at being disturbed. He wore jeans—none too clean—and a faded flannel shirt hanging unbuttoned over a dingy white undershirt.

"Yeah? What do you want?"

"A few words with Mrs. Shirley Dwyer. Does she live here?"

"Yeah, Ma lives here."

I held out my card. He opened the screen door just wide enough to take it. He read it slowly, as if sounding out each syllable.

Then he looked at me, disbelief in his eyes. "You're a private investigator? You sure don't look like one."

Though I wondered what he thought a PI looked like, I didn't ask.

"What do you want with Ma?"

"A little information."

"About what?"

If I didn't give him the right answer, he'd slam the door in my face. I decided to go with the truth. "About Mrs. MacNiall."

"That witch? Did she finally decide to reopen the factory?"

"What factory?"

"The one she closed without warning just before Christmas, throwing four hundred people out of work."

Rose MacNiall had laid off people just before Christmas? That was truly cold-blooded. "I don't know anything about the factory," I said apologetically.

"Who is it, Rodney?" a voice called from inside the house.

"Nobody, Ma."

"Mrs. Dwyer? Could I speak with you?" I asked loudly. Rodney pushed the door shut. A minute later he opened it with a morose look at me and motioned me inside.

The front door opened right into the living room. Not wanting to track snow onto the highly polished hardwood floor, I remained standing on the welcome mat.

An old woman in a wheelchair faced me from the middle of the room. "Come on in," she said.

I unzipped my boots and left them on the mat. As I started toward her, two big dogs bounded into the room and headed straight for me. I let out a small yelp of alarm.

"Down!" Rodney yelled. "Sit," he commanded.

Reluctantly, it seemed to me, the dogs sat in front of the coffee table, keeping their alert eyes on me.

"They won't hurt you," Rodney said. "They're lovers, not fighters. Worthless as watch dogs. If they weren't such good bird dogs, I'd have gotten rid of 'em long ago."

Why did it not surprise me that he was a hunter? He probably owned several weapons and was a fierce opponent of gun control.

Perhaps sensing my apprehension, Shirley asked her son to take the dogs out.

It's not that I didn't like dogs. I did, but the only one I'd ever been close to was Maxi's dog, Hiram, who is small and well-mannered. He always waited for me to make the first move, and he never pounced on me.

I glanced around. The living room featured the usual sectional sofa and a recliner facing a large-screen television set. The fireplace was obviously working. It's only decoration were two crossed swords affixed above the mantel. They looked like the ones worn by officers in Civil War movies, only deadly real. As mantel decorations I much preferred vases of flowers or candles, but to each his own.

"What can I do for you?" Shirley asked.

"Do you remember Mrs. Rose MacNiall?" I thought Shirley's face lost what little color it had.

"Who could forget that woman? Cold as ice and tough as old shoe leather."

"She hired your professional services as midwife to attend her daughter Liza. Right?"

Shirley nodded. "Actually, it was the grandmother— Miss Patricia as everyone called her—who hired me. She was even worse than Rose." Shirley shuddered.

"Tell me about them."

"Seventeen-year-old girl, scared to death. The labor went on too long. I begged Mrs. Rose to send for a doctor. She might have done it, but her mother-in-law, Miss Patricia, forbade it. What a witch that woman was. She would have let that girl die, but her father, bless him, went behind her back and called a doctor. Not the family doctor, mind you, but one who had lost his license. Still, the man had delivered his share of babies, and together we managed and saved the mother's life."

"You said Liza's life was in danger?"

"Yeah. We almost lost her. And I'm pretty sure she can't have any more children."

A heavy price to pay for fake respectability.

"I know this happened a long time ago, but do you remember the doctor's name?"

She nodded. "Dr. Gideon."

"How do you remember this so clearly?"

"He'd been in some trouble over amphetamines. News like that gets around among the medical profession."

"According to Liza, you arranged for the baby's adoption." I hadn't thought it possible for the woman to grow paler, but she did.

"Who told you that?" she whispered.

"Liza."

"I'm surprised she remembered anything from that night."

"She said you'd been nice to her." I watched tears rise in her eyes. Embarrassed, she brushed them away.

"I always felt bad about that case. But what could I have done? The girl was a minor. I couldn't see any signs of her being mistreated. She lived in this beautiful house . . ." Her voice trailed off.

"What happened to the baby?"

"Is that what this is about? Liza wants to find her?"

"No. Her mother does."

Shirley's mouth dropped open. "That doesn't make any sense. Rose was the one who insisted that I take the baby away and get her adopted."

"To whom did you give the baby?"

Shirley shook her head. "I can't tell you that."

"Can't or won't?"

"Can't."

"Years ago adoption records were sealed but the laws have changed," I pointed out.

"Well, then you shouldn't have any trouble finding the baby."

She said that rather glibly. Something was wrong. Mentally I ticked off the various possibilities. Finally I said, "You can't sell a baby. Not even on the black market. You can't sell human beings. We fought a civil war over this issue." I paused. "Or was it two babies you sold?"

I watched the color drain from her face. Then she clutched her chest and started to wheeze. The wheezing grew worse. She dug into the pocket of her house dress but came up empty.

"What do you need? An inhaler?"

She nodded, trying to get air into her lungs. I looked around but couldn't spot the inhaler. I ran in the direction I had seen her son go. Flinging open the back door, I yelled his name.

He came running. "What's wrong?"

"Your mother needs her inhaler."

He rushed past me. I followed more slowly. By the time I reached the living room, Shirley was breathing through the inhaler. Rodney was bent over her, watching. Having caused the attack, I felt like a criminal. I edged toward the door.

"You better leave," he said, straightening up. "Ma suffers from asthma. Getting her upset can bring on an attack."

"I'm sorry," I said. "Will she be okay?"

"Yes."

"I'm glad, but I still need that information. Please think about it, Mrs. Dwyer." I pulled on my boots.

She looked at me, and I thought she gave a small nod.

"I'll be back," I said, but my delivery lacked the oomph that made the movie hero's line so memorable.

By the time I returned to town, it was after five. Since Lynn would have locked up the office, I drove home. Halfway there, I remembered my bare refrigerator. I could have made do with peanut butter and crackers but the kitten I'd inherited on a previous case needed something more suitable.

I didn't trust the convenience store I passed on the way home to have the kitten chow Buddy liked, so I made a U-turn and headed for my regular grocery store. Naturally, I didn't have my list with me, so I'd probably remember only half the items I needed. By the time I was done, I had a lot more groceries than I'd anticipated, including a potted basil plant, which smelled heavenly.

Somebody had dropped a bag of groceries in the vestibule right in front of the community bulletin board.

While I waited for the family to pick up the scattered items, I amused myself by reading the handwritten messages on the board. Someone was selling a set of teacups with matching teapot, embroidered place mats with napkins, and a new toaster. Wedding presents or shower gifts from a union fallen apart before it was ever joined? The thought made me sad. Someone was offering an Elvis statue but failed to say with or without a guitar. Then there was a stationary bike, probably bought with the New Year's resolution of exercising more, and a two-wheeled club cart.

My eyes moved on before the name on the last notice hit me. R. Gideon. Could this be the Ralph Gideon I was looking for? I couldn't afford not to check this out. I copied the phone number and hurriedly wheeled my cart of groceries to my car. I dialed the number and silently thanked whoever invented cell phones.

A woman's voice answered. She pronounced "hello" as if it were spelled "yellow."

"I'm trying to reach R. Gideon who advertised a club cart for sale. Is this the right number?"

"Yeah. Hang on."

Without covering the mouthpiece, she hollered for someone named Jack and told him to get Ralph.

"It'll take a while. Ralph lives two trailers down and he don't move so fast no more," she said.

"That's okay. I'll hold." Trailer. If memory served me right, Westport had at least three trailer parks. "Are you in the park near the airport?"

"Heavens, no. Way too noisy with them planes landing and taking off at all hours. We're on the old Minton Road, just before it becomes Route 3. You know the big cemetery? We're right next to it."

Route 3 was beginning to haunt me. Vaguely I remembered driving past a large cemetery.

"Here's Ralph."

We spoke briefly. The club cart was still available. We agreed on a price should I like it and arranged for me to see it in the morning.

During the night it had snowed again, making driving a little hazardous. Snow at the end of February wasn't unusual in our part of the country, but I was getting tired of it. Proceeding slowly, I prayed not to have to slam on the brakes for any reason and go into a wild spin. It took a while, but I made it safely to the trailer park. A young man was busily plowing the driveways. I parked in the spot he indicated and made my way to the trailer he'd pointed out. My tracks were the only thing marring the blindingly white surface.

Ralph Gideon must have been watching for me. He opened the door before I had a chance to knock. I stepped on the newspaper he'd spread on the floor just inside the trailer, which was an old model. Only one room wide, the living room was on my right, the bedroom and bath on my left, and the kitchen was the tiny area around the front door. The place was tidy and clean.

"The cart's right here," he said.

A small, trim man, he shuffled toward the cart which he'd leaned against a loudly humming, avocado-colored refrigerator.

"It's collapsible, as you can see." He then proceeded to unfold it.

"It looks good. Dr. Gideon, I need to ask you some questions."

He turned, a disappointed look on his face. "Then this was just a ruse? You're not interested in the golf cart?"

"Oh, I am interested. I've got the check ready for you," I said and took it out of my purse. I laid it on the kitchen counter. He picked it up, looked at it, then carefully folded it and put it into the pocket of his cardigan. I noticed that one of the brown buttons had been sewn on with white thread, an endearing touch, showing he cared enough to be tidy but not enough to be vain.

"The cart's for my husband." That was true as I didn't play golf, but Luke was just starting to take lessons at in indoor driving range. I knew he hadn't acquired all the necessary equipment, so I was going to give him the cart for his birthday. He always remembered my birthday, so I felt compelled to remember his with a gift as well.

"What do you want to ask me?"

"Seventeen years ago you were called by the Mac-Nialls to assist in the birth of their teenaged daughter's baby."

He sighed. "I knew that some day this was going to come back to bite me in the rear."

"And why's that?"

"I'd had trouble with them before over their son and because there was something funny about the whole thing. Slightly off. I wasn't their doctor, nor was I an OB-GYN. Why call me? Made no sense."

"Why did you go?"

"Curiosity and because Miss Patricia could still have caused me more trouble. And because I still retained traces of my training, which stipulated that a doctor had to treat the patient in front of him."

"Can you be more specific about something not being right?"

"Why do you want to know?"

I handed him my card. "I've been hired by Rose Mac-Niall to find the baby that was born that night."

"Babies."

I did a double take. "Babies? As in more than one?"

"Mind you, I didn't actually see two babies, but from what I saw, I delivered the second baby. I was called in too late to deliver the first."

"Wouldn't the mother know she'd given birth to twins?"

"Not necessarily. The labor had been long and she'd been given some strong medication. I doubt that she remembered much of anything that happened that night."

"What did the MacNialls tell you? Surely they must have known that you suspected something?"

"Miss Patricia poured me a glass of fine cognac afterwards and told me to sign a form that I had delivered one baby girl that night. Then she handed me a fistful of cash that far exceeded any normal delivery fee. I needed the money desperately, and I *had* only delivered one baby." He shrugged.

"And you never told this to anyone?"

"Nobody every asked me and, as far as I know, no crime was committed. The MacNialls are a powerful family and people with power and money get away with things us ordinary mortals don't. You probably never met Miss Patricia. Now that was one scary woman." He shuddered a little.

"What do you think happened to the first baby?"

Again he shrugged. "Something must have gone wrong. But I'm sure not even Miss Patricia would kill a newborn."

"But why hide the fact that the baby was born in the first place?"

"Questions would have been asked. From what Miss Patricia said, the baby I delivered would be secretly adopted and nobody would know that her granddaughter had disgraced the family."

"She actually used the word *disgraced?*"

"Yes. I felt sorry for the granddaughter."

"What would they have done with the body?" I wondered out loud.

"Give it to someone to dispose of or . . ." He paused and rubbed his ear. "Have you been to the MacNiall estate?"

"No."

"It's huge. Surrounded by its own park and a tall stone wall. Lots of places for a small grave."

Though the trailer was very warm, I suddenly shivered. "Did you ever treat any of the MacNialls later?"

He laughed mirthlessly. "I once ran into Miss Patricia at the library, and she looked through me as if I were a pane of glass. To her way of thinking, she had paid me well and bought my silence and that was the end of it."

"Do you have any idea who might have adopted the baby?"

"No. But I'll bet my stethoscope which my sainted mother gave me that the adoption was *not* handled through a legitimate agency."

"So finding the baby will be difficult."

"I would think so. I did notice that the baby had a birthmark on the inside of her upper left arm. Halfway between the elbow and the shoulder."

"Was it the kind of birthmark that might have been removed later in life?" I asked.

"I doubt that. It was just a small patch of light brown skin discoloration, about the size of a penny. It wasn't unsightly or dangerous."

"Is there anything else you can tell me that would help me find the baby?"

"My guess is that they used an illegal adoption service."

"You must have some idea who ran the illegal adoptions?"

"Suspicions, yes. Facts and proof, no."

"I'd be grateful for your suspicions."

"There were a couple of midwives—sisters—who

lived in the last house on London Street. I can't remember the exact address, but the house was on the left-hand side, just before you get to the railroad crossing."

"You remember their names?"

"Yeah. Washington. Latisha and Janaya or Janiann. Something like that. And you might try the nurse. She seemed to be on more intimate terms with the family."

"Shirley Dwyer?"

"That's the name. You know her?"

"I spoke with her, but I had the feeling she wasn't telling me everything she knew."

He nodded. "I saw her a few months later that year and she was driving an expensive, late-model car. I wondered if she, too, had been paid with a handful of cash." He started toward the door, signaling that our talk was over.

I picked up the collapsible cart and left.

Chapter Three

Uncle Barney was back. I knew that by the scent of his sweet pipe tobacco. That he had already lit his pipe by eight in the morning was not a good sign.

"He's busy," Lynn snapped as soon as I walked into the agency.

Fortunately he saw me through his open door and asked me to come into his office.

"I understand we have a new client," he said, and motioned me to a chair.

I closed the door before I sat down. "Yes, we do. It's a missing persons case, and I'm not sure I should have taken it."

"Did you guarantee the client that we'd find the missing person?"

"Of course not. I wouldn't do that even if I thought the case was going to be easy."

"And this one isn't? Tell me about it."

So I did. In detail.

"What strikes you as especially difficult?"

"Everyone I've talked to has lied to me or omitted important stuff—"

"Clients, unfortunately, almost always do that. What else?"

"The time span. Seventeen years have passed since one baby was adopted and the other one—"

"If in fact there *were* two babies."

I nodded. "Dr. Gideon said he never saw two babies but yet he's sure there were two."

Barney nodded. "You probably don't know this, but Dr. Gideon was involved in an illegal amphetamine distribution scandal. Lost his license to practice. The MacNialls played a leading role in this. He may have a personal ax to grind."

"Their son overdosed on speed and they blame Dr. Gideon for this?"

"Yes."

"Nice to have someone to blame other than yourself."

"Isn't it." Barney emptied the tobacco out of his pipe. "What was your impression of Rose MacNiall?"

"In appearance she reminded me of the English actress who played Miss Marple. The first actress. The one who portrayed her in the films, not on television. Margaret something."

"Rutherford. Margaret Rutherford."

"That's right." Uncle Barney shared my and Luke's love of old movies. "She even wore a cape, but there was nothing dithery or benign about Rose. That's one tough woman."

"And does that intimidate us?" he asked with a raised eyebrow.

"No, but she is a little daunting."

"I'll talk with her. Phone her to come in."

I could tell by the slight grin pulling at the corner of his mouth that Uncle Barney looked forward to locking horns with the formidable Rozalia.

From my office I phoned the number she had left. A secretary or assistant told me that Mrs. MacNiall was slightly indisposed and could not leave the house. Could we call on her?

I went back to Uncle Barney's office and told him.

"You look like you want to go," he said.

"I've always wondered what that mansion looked like on the inside, haven't you?" From the look he shot me, I could tell he had not. Maybe this curiosity about interiors was a woman thing.

Glancing at his calendar, he said, "I'm free this afternoon after three. Find out if she can see us then."

After I held up my ID to the camera for the guard to see, the wrought iron gate swung open. Uncle Barney drove through it and parked under the porte cochere which flanked the right side of the mansion.

During the lengthy curving drive up to the house I had a chance to admire it. Built from Indiana stone whose colors varied subtly, it featured six fireplace chimneys. Most of the windows were Romanesque which, along with the round tower in back, gave the building an aura of fortresslike invulnerability.

I started to get out of the car when vicious barking caused me to swing my legs back in and slam the door shut. I even locked it though I doubted the two big dogs snarling at me could open it, but I wasn't taking a chance. The sound of a thin, high whistle made them back up. Moments later the guard came running, clipped leashes to their collars, apologized, and led them away. My heartbeat returned to normal. I pitied the person who came here uninvited.

"Think it's safe to get out?"

Uncle Barney nodded and led the way.

I enjoyed letting the heavy iron metal knocker hit the double door to announce our arrival, just in case the dogs' barking had failed to do so. Long minutes passed before the door was opened by an elderly, chubby, and very short woman who must have reached way up over her head to grasp the heavy handle. Uncle Barney told her we were expected. She didn't say a word, glared at us grumpily for interrupting her day, and with an impatient hand gesture motioned us to follow her.

Since the housekeeper walked, or rather waddled, very slowly, I had a chance to look around. Through a back window I glimpsed a swimming pool covered with a blue tarp and a tennis court. Beyond them a big garden spread to the high stone wall that enclosed it. Come spring it would be a lovely place. Toward the back I saw a hot house and a shed.

The entrance hall was huge with a high ceiling and a massive oak staircase at the far end. The posts were intricately carved with a pineapple motif. The two fireplaces bore traces of cold ashes. A few beige-gray tapestries hung on the walls, the only decorative touches in the cold room. I suspected they were imported from France or Belgium.

The woman led us to Rose MacNiall's office. She sat behind a large oak desk. A small rug—the kind used to keep warm in horse-drawn buggies—covered her knees and a crocheted shawl was draped over her shoulders. I glanced at her hands, half expecting her to be wearing wool gloves with the fingertips cut off. This room, too, was cold. The only source of heat I could detect was a small space heater. Why was she so parsimonious with the heat? Granted the house had to be expensive to heat, but surely she could afford it.

The man sitting at a smaller desk rose politely. He was tall, with a finely chiseled profile and thick, gray hair brushed straight back. Rose introduced him as Francis MacNiall, her late husband's cousin and a vice president of MacNiall Industries. We shook hands. He remained standing, as did we. Rose didn't invite us to sit.

"Do you have anything to report to me?" Rose asked.

"It's the other way around. You need to report to us, level with us," Barney said.

"What are you talking about? I hired you to find my granddaughter."

"Why?"

"What do you mean, why?" she demanded.

"You couldn't get rid of her fast enough seventeen years ago."

"That was then, and this is now."

Talk about using clichés.

We both stared at Rose, but from the mulish set of her mouth I knew she wasn't going to cooperate. She wasn't going to tell us the real reason for suddenly wanting Chelsea in her life.

"We'll do our best to find your granddaughter," Barney told her, "but our job would be a lot easier and we'd get speedier results if you told us the truth."

"It's not my task to make your job easier," she snapped, her tone waspish.

I could see the muscle next to Uncle Barney's left eye twitch and knew he was tightly controlling his temper.

"We'll report to you in a couple of weeks. If you think of anything helpful, please call," I said and quickly took Uncle Barney's arm. I got us out of there fast.

As soon as we were outside, I asked, "Do you believe for a moment that she wants Chelsea back out of familial affection?"

He shot me a sideways look and grunted. That was a definite no.

"I doubt that woman felt deep affection for anyone in her entire life," he said.

"Does she want the girl back out of guilt?"

"Doubtful. She doesn't strike me as the type of person who suffers greatly from guilt."

"Out of a sudden sense of responsibility?" I asked.

"Also doubtful."

"Then why?" I asked, frustrated.

"That's the crucial question, but I'm absolutely sure the reason has nothing to do with ethics, sentiment, or grandmotherly affection."

"Money? Property?" I guessed.

"I think we can safely assume that. We need to find out what's in James MacNiall's will."

I nodded. "I wonder if we might get something out of Francis MacNiall."

"Leave him to me. I'll do some checking to see what I can find out about him."

Then it hit me. "I know someone who might tell us if she knows. And being his daughter and Chelsea's mother, Liza should know what's in her father's will, shouldn't she?"

"Yes. Unless she was written out of it."

"I don't think so. It's only her mother and grandmother that Liza was at odds with. I got the impression that she got along with her father."

"Then please get in touch with her as soon as possible."

That's what I did. Again I waited outside her apartment building. I paced to keep warm. When I saw her approach, I walked toward her.

"I need to talk to you. Want to get a cup of coffee?"

"After the day I had, I need something stronger. Buy me a martini at the Westport Bar and you've got a deal."

"Do we walk or drive?"

"It's just a couple of blocks west of here. Hard to find a parking place there."

We walked in silence to the bar.

"Your usual?" the bartender asked Liza when we sat at the bar.

"Yeah, but use the good gin. She's buying."

"Okay. What'll you have, miss?"

"A club soda with a lime twist. I'm still working." Why I felt the need to justify my choice of drink, I didn't know.

We watched him mix the martini with a flourish.

Liza took a tiny sip, tasting it. She nodded in approval. "Oh yeah. This is good." She took a healthy slug, lit a cigarette, and turned toward me. "What do you want to know?"

I hesitated for a moment. Intuitively I knew it was wrong to ask her about her father's will right off the bat. "What can you tell me about Francis MacNiall?"

"You've met Uncle Francis? Well, he's okay. Or would be if he hadn't been under my grandmother's thumb or if he weren't my mother's hatchet man now. And he's got a wicked temper, especially when someone calls him Fran, which my mom sometimes does."

He hadn't struck me as hatchet man material, but then he hadn't said much, and not all hatchet men looked like they belonged in an Al Capone film.

"I don't mean he rubs out people the way they do in the movies."

"He fires people?"

"Oh, no. My mother likes doing that herself. He does his bloodletting around the negotiation table. You might have read in the papers that the workers at MacNiall Industries have been on strike for over two months? Well, Uncle Francis is in charge of the negotiations with the union. It's his job to give the workers as little as possible so that the MacNialls can keep most of the filthy lucre for themselves. Not that they need it. They have more than enough to last several lifetimes."

She sighed and stubbed out her cigarette. She took another sip of her martini before she continued. "When my father was alive, he looked out for his workers."

The perfect lead-in to her father's will. "Liza, we're still trying to find out why your mother hired us to find your daughter." And only one daughter. Rose must know what happened to the other baby. "Can you and will you tell us what's in your father's will?"

"I can't. At least not yet. The reading of the will isn't until next week. I've been invited. Probably so Mother can gloat when I get nothing."

"I had the impression that you got along okay with your dad."

Liza nodded. "We'd begun speaking again. We'd even made plans to have lunch together, but he died. *C'est la vie.*" She drained her drink.

"I'm sorry."

"Yeah, me too."

"Can we meet after the reading of the will?"

"Sure. Give me a call."

"Would you like another drink?"

"I'd love one."

I ordered her another martini. "Would you like something to eat? A sandwich? Fries? Chips?"

Liza giggled. "Don't worry. Two drinks won't get me drunk. Besides, I'm walking, not driving. But I will take some chips."

I'd have preferred it if she'd ordered a sandwich, but reminded myself that nobody had appointed me the nutrition police. I paid our bill and left.

Knowing that Uncle Barney would still be at the agency, I drove back to work.

Uncle Barney was in his office.

"I have good news and bad news," I told him. "The bad news is that the reading of the will is not until next week, and the good news is that Liza will tell me what's in the will. She's been invited to attend."

"Good."

"What do we do in the meantime?"

"I'm meeting Francis MacNiall this evening."

"Liza says he's Rose's hatchet man and is dominated by her just as he used to be by Miss Patricia."

"I'm not surprised. It would take a grimly determined man to continuously stand up to two such strong, ruthless women."

"What do you want me to do? Go see Shirley Dwyer again and see if I can get her to talk about how many babies were born that night and what happened to them?"

"If there really were two babies and one of them died and she didn't report it, or if she used a black market adoption agency that paid her, she could still face charges, even though a lot of time has passed."

"Are you saying I probably won't get anything out of her?"

"At this point nobody could. We have no leverage." Barney thought for a moment. "But it won't hurt to rattle her cage and see what happens. If she meets someone. If someone comes to see her."

"Surveillance?"

Barney nodded.

"I'll have to find a spot from where I can watch the house. I can't get too close because of the dogs."

"And if the hog's gone, you'll know the son isn't there."

It took a second before I remembered that Harley-Davidson bikes were affectionately referred to as hogs.

"That brand of motorcycle isn't cheap, is it?" I asked.

"No."

"And their SUV is new."

"They could have financed it," Barney pointed out.

"Rodney's been laid off and Shirley's retired or disabled. Their house is large and in good condition with a big yard. Maybe even some acreage behind it. Even if both were working, doesn't it seem to you that they're living above their means?"

Barney nodded. "That had occurred to me too. Dr. Gideon freely admitted that he'd received a large fee. I bet it was a one-time payment."

"And that's why he told us, because there was nothing illegal about it. What if Shirley keeps receiving money? That would explain how they can afford their lifestyle."

"Blackmail."

We sat in silence, considering this possibility. Next to murder, blackmail seemed to be a particularly ugly crime. It was built on fear and guilt. "You once told me that eventually the victim gets tired of being blackmailed."

"True. If the blackmailer is smart, he or she will know when to quit or at least keep the money demands reasonable."

"But greed being what it is—"

"Yes," Barney said. "Greed usually wins out over prudence and common sense."

"It occurred to me that the adoptive parents must have filed for a birth certificate. Every child needs one sooner or later. We know the baby was a female, we know the date of birth and the county, as well as the doctor's name. It might take some time to search the databases, but it'll be worth it. You want me to do it?"

Barney shook his head. "I need you and Glenn on stake-out duty."

"Twenty-four hours?"

"No. Once the Dwyers are in for the night, there's no

sense sitting out in the cold and the dark. Glenn is still out on another case, so can you take the morning shift?"

"No problem."

No problem wasn't exactly true, I discovered the next morning. Surveillance out in the country in deep winter wasn't easy. A car parked for any length of time on a snowy country road was bound to arouse curiosity. I had to find a place from which I could observe the house while at the same time conceal the Jeep I'd borrowed from the agency.

I found no hiding place east of the Dwyer home so I had to drive past the house. About a half mile west a farm road led to a stand of trees. I backed the Jeep as far behind the trees as I dared without running the risk of getting stuck in the snow. I placed the binoculars on the dashboard. Though I could see the house, I was too far away to see a visitor clearly or read the license plate on a vehicle.

Although I wore a full-length parka, fur-lined boots and heavy tights under my jeans and a turtleneck under the warm pullover Maxi had knitted for me, it was cold enough that I had to run the engine from time to time. I prayed I was far enough from the house that the noise of the motor couldn't be heard. I was also counting on Rodney's predilection for watching television with the volume on high.

When Glenn came to take the next shift, I was thirsty, hungry, bored, and needed to use the bathroom.

"Anything going on?" Glenn asked.

"Rodney left at ten and hasn't returned yet. I'm surprised he left his mother alone that long."

"She may be in a wheelchair, but that doesn't mean she's helpless. And Rodney? Maybe he got a job."

"Has the MacNiall plant resumed production?"

"No, but I was thinking maybe he'd taken a minimum wage job somewhere to make ends meet. Unemployment benefits aren't exactly generous."

Grateful for being relieved from surveillance duty, I got into my car and drove home. I felt stiff and sluggish from sitting all those hours, yet the idea of swimming laps in a cool pool only made me shiver.

Then I remembered the flyer in my mailbox about aerobic exercise sessions at the Westport Community Center. I drove home, changed into exercise gear, and joined a group of some twenty leotard-clad woman led by a young and very energetic instructor.

Sixty sweaty minutes later I showered in the locker room and drove home. I almost stopped for fast food, but remembered the macaroni-cheese-broccoli casserole Maxi had fixed for me.

While I ate, Glenn phoned.

"We got some activity. Finally."

"Yeah? What's happening?"

"A black Lincoln drove up to the house. Someone got out on the passenger side and went into the house. I timed the visit. It lasted exactly five-and-a-half minutes. The figure came out, got into the back seat, and the car drove off."

"I know it was too dark to see clearly, but can you describe the figure?"

"Stocky build. Wearing a cape and a hat. I'd say it was an elderly woman from the careful way she walked on the snow-covered path to the door, but beyond that I can't elaborate."

"Your description and the Lincoln suggest that it was Rose MacNiall. I wonder what she wanted from Shirley."

"I couldn't even guess since I haven't met either woman," Glenn said.

"You haven't missed much. Neither of them bears the slightest resemblance to Mother Teresa."

"How long do you want me to stay here?"

"Has Rodney come home yet?"

"No."

"There's a snow advisory in effect until after midnight. I think you should leave within the hour. Don't get stuck out there."

"I won't."

While I ate my dinner, I kept thinking about the connection between the two women. Seventeen years ago they shared a . . . what? Secret? An illegal act? Whatever it had been, it was the only thing they had in common, but it had to be something powerful to maintain even a tenuous bond between them.

I had to admit after a while that I just didn't have enough facts to keep on brooding, so I fed Buddy and went to bed. She followed me after she ate and performed her elaborate grooming routine. I fell asleep while she was still washing her face.

Next morning it took a good hour to shovel my sidewalk and dig out the Jeep. Though the weatherman maintained it had snowed only six inches, it seemed to me like twice that much.

Afterwards I rewarded myself with a cinnamon roll and two cups of coffee. Thus fortified, I drove to my stakeout.

Though the highway had been plowed, the country roads hadn't. I thought I detected traces of tire marks on the road, but they were faint, as if they'd been made during the snow storm.

Both vehicles sat in the Dwyer's driveway. No attempt had been made to clear off the snow. The light over the front door was still on. I was almost past the house before it hit me that something was wrong. Nobody left their front door open in our kind of winter.

I slammed on the brakes, which was a dumb thing to do, as it sent me into a fishtail spin that turned the car almost all the way around. I was lucky not to have ended up in the ditch. My heart thudded heavily from the near mishap. Slowly, I drove back and stopped the car behind the motorcycle.

I debated with myself what to do. If I walked up to the house to tell them that their front door was open behind the screen door and they said they were airing out the house, I'd feel like a fool. But if something was wrong and I didn't check, I'd never forgive myself. Better to feel foolish than to feel guilty. And where were the dogs? Shouldn't they be barking their heads off when a stranger approached the house?

I walked to the door and rang the bell. No one responded.

"Hello? Mrs. Dwyer? Rodney?"

No answer, but I now heard the faint barking of the dogs as if they were in the back part of the house.

"Hello? Anybody home?"

Tentatively I pulled at the screen door. It opened. I called again, and then cautiously stepped inside.

Seconds later, I wished I hadn't.

I staggered back and pressed my hands over my mouth to keep from throwing up.

"Oh, please, no," I heard before I realized it was my whimpered plea. I ran outside. Still fighting nausea, I scooped up some snow and pressed it against my face. I thought my legs might collapse, but I made it to the Jeep and my cell phone. I had Uncle Barney on speed dial. He answered.

"So much blood. I can't believe there's that much blood," I said, my voice as shaky as my legs.

"Cybil, where are you?"

"At the Dwyer house."

"And where's the blood?"

"In the living room."

"Are the Dwyers there?"

"On the floor, lying in the blood."

"Cybil, are you sure they're dead?"

"Yes. The blood's already gotten thicker and darker."

"Hang on. I'll call nine-one-one."

"No, I better do it. Can you call Sam?"

"Sam works for the city police. The county's in the sheriff's jurisdiction. I'll phone him."

I dialed 911. I must confess that my report was less than coherent, but the operator was patient and guided me through a series of questions until she had the information she needed.

She told me to go sit in my car until help arrived. I was only too happy to do that. I sat there, my arms wrapped around myself, shivering uncontrollably even though I had cranked up the Jeep's heater.

The sheriff's car arrived first. He parked behind the SUV. I got out and waited for him. I pointed toward the front door. "In there."

He nodded and went into the house. He came back out almost immediately. Using his car radio, he asked for backup and demanded to know where the ambulance was. Then he came and stood beside me.

"You called nine-one-one?"

"Yes. I also called my uncle, Barney Keller. And he called you."

"Did you see anyone?"

"No. I only stepped inside the door. I didn't look anywhere else. The dogs? Where are the dogs?"

"We'll look for them. Don't worry about them."

The ambulance arrived, followed by a couple of squad cars, the coroner's van, and Uncle Barney. He took me to his car where I told him and the sheriff everything I remembered from the moment I arrived.

A deputy came from around the back of the house, leading the dogs which he reported had been in one of the back bedrooms.

"Take them to the pound for the time being," the sheriff said.

"They're good bird dogs." Both men looked at me. "Rodney told me. I can't believe he's dead. That they're both dead. Shirley was in a wheelchair, practically helpless." Uncle Barney patted my shoulder.

We sat in silence until the coroner came out. Uncle Barney rolled down the window.

The sheriff asked, "Doc, what can you tell us? Time of death? Weapons used? Anything?"

"Time of death? Mind you this is just a rough guess at this point. Sometime late last night. The weapon? A long, fairly thin blade, but strong enough to hack somebody to death with it."

"Like the swords over the fireplace," I whispered, and then bolted from the car. I rounded the hedge before I became violently sick to my stomach.

Chapter Four

Uncle Barney sent me home. I couldn't blame him, not after I'd disgraced myself by throwing up. My only consolation was that both he and the sheriff had looked a little gray-green after viewing the murder scene.

At home, I tried lying down but couldn't stay put. I turned the television on but when all I could see was the blood and the bodies, I turned it off. I couldn't concentrate on the novel I'd found so interesting the evening before. I picked up my knitting but kept dropping stitches, so I put it down. All I could do successfully was pace the floor.

Buddy, my one-eyed kitten, sat and watched with the patience only cats possess, her one golden eye never even blinking. Until the doorbell rang. Then she ran and sat behind the umbrella stand. From there she could see the door without being seen clearly herself.

Luke. He was wearing scrubs, so I knew he'd come straight from the hospital.

"Let me guess. Uncle Barney called you. Aren't you on duty?"

"I get a lunch break just like everybody else."

Looking at my watch, I said, "At eleven in the morning?"

"We're flexible unless there's an emergency, and right now the only emergency is you. May I come in?"

"Why not. You're here," I muttered rather gloomily.

"Have you had lunch?" Luke asked.

"Please. I may never eat again. I don't think I could keep anything down."

"That's understandable, but you have to drink something. Can't let you get dehydrated. Come to the kitchen with me."

Without waiting for my reply, Luke grabbed my hand and pulled me after him. He opened the refrigerator. "Tomato juice?"

"No! It's red. Like blood."

"Sorry, bad choice. Orange juice. It's got sugar for energy and tons of vitamins." He poured a glass and set it on the table. "Drink."

He was in his chief-of-the-emergency-room persona and protest would have been futile. I took a tiny sip. When it stayed down, I took another.

"Good girl."

"There was so much blood. How could there have been so much blood?" I asked, looking at him.

"The average adult body contains about ten pints of blood. So when exsanguination occurs—that is, when someone bleeds out—that's a lot of the red stuff being spilled."

I shuddered and swayed. Instantly his arms enfolded me and held me.

"I'm so sorry you had to stumble on that scene."

A knock followed by the sound of a key in the kitchen door told me my grandmother had arrived.

"You phoned Maxi?"

"Yes. I have to go back to work and if I hadn't called her, she'd have never forgiven me. You think I'd risk never eating any of her apfelstrudel again?"

I had to smile a little.

"That's better," Luke said and kissed me on the forehead before we both turned toward the door to welcome Maxi.

"My poor Schatzi. Why is it always you who has to find the dead?"

She put her arms around me, and I immediately felt a little better.

"I brought lunch. Can you stay, Luke?"

"Unfortunately not."

"I was afraid of that so I made yours to go."

Luke's face lit up. "Bless you, Maxi. What did you bring?"

"The vegetable soup you like and tuna salad on homemade whole wheat bread."

"I've died and gone to heaven." Luke accepted the thermos and the brown paper bag containing his sandwich.

"The soup will stay hot for another couple of hours. Of course it can be reheated and still taste okay."

Ever gallant, Luke said, "It would even taste great cold." He bent down and kissed her cheek before he left.

Maxi watched him leave and sighed. She turned to me and said, "Well?"

"Well, what?"

"Anything happening between Luke and you?"

"No. Uncle Barney called him to check on me. That's all."

"What a shame, but be warned. I'm not writing you two off yet. And don't roll your eyes," Maxi said.

"Would I do something that juvenile?" I asked, even as I'd been tempted to do just that.

"Are you staying home today?"

"No. I have to see two midwives who allegedly ran an illegal adoption agency."

"I'm going with you," Maxi said.

"Why?"

"Because I know the Washington sisters and you don't."

My mouth dropped open. "How did you know it was them?"

"Westport is a small town. And they are, or rather were, the only game in town."

"So it wasn't exactly a secret what they did?"

"Not really, but they were careful and kept a low profile."

"Is it because illegal adoption is one of those victimless crimes?" I asked, moving my fingers to indicate quotation marks around victimless crimes.

"I guess most of the time it seems like a victimless crime."

"Unless the couple who receives the baby turns out to be irresponsible. Then the baby becomes the victim."

"That's why we have carefully regulated agencies who make sure that this doesn't happen," Maxi pointed out.

We drove in separate cars to the London Street address. We waited quite a while on the porch after I'd rung the doorbell. If I hadn't seen the lace curtain in one of the downstairs windows move, I'd have thought that nobody was home. Finally the door opened.

A stick-thin woman glanced briefly at me but stared at Maxi.

"Hello, Letty. It's been a long time."

"Sure has, Miz Keller."

"This is my granddaughter, Cybil Quindt."

We exchanged pleased-to-meet yous.

"Is your sister at home?" Maxi asked.

"Jane Ann hasn't been well, but she likes company. Please come on in."

Jane Ann lay on the sofa, her large body propped up by several pillows. A walker stood next to the sofa.

Introductions and greetings over, Maxi got to business.

"I want you to think back seventeen years. Shirley

Dwyer brought you a baby, maybe two, to place for adoption. The adoption may have been irregular or not. That doesn't matter to us. We need to know who adopted the baby or babies."

I watched the sisters look at each other with alarm.

"Why don't you ask Shirley Dwyer," Letty finally said.

"We can't. She's dead," I said.

"Oh dear. I didn't see her obituary in the paper, and I always read the obituaries carefully," Jane Ann said.

"You'll read about her death in tonight's paper, but it'll be on the front page." I hadn't meant to blurt out the news of Shirley's death quite so bluntly and looked apologetically at Maxi, who didn't seem to be upset with me.

"Mercy me. Are you sure?" Jane Ann asked.

"Unfortunately, yes. I found her body." Both women looked at me in shock.

"Why on the front page?" Jane Ann asked.

"Because she didn't die peacefully in her bed."

Letty gasped while her sister clutched the collar of her robe.

"And you think her death has got something to do with the adoptions?" Jane Ann asked.

I shrugged. "I have no proof, but it's a monumental coincidence that she died just after I asked her about the adoption."

"I mistrust coincidences," Maxi said.

Jane Ann motioned her sister to her side and whispered something in her ear. Letty nodded.

"We're retired midwives and know nothing about illegal adoptions," Jane Ann said.

"That's right," her sister chimed in, "and we know nothing. We'd like for you all to leave now." Letty made a shooing motion with her hands.

Maxi shook her head sadly. "Such lies and both of you churchgoing women. I am disappointed in you."

Nobody could lay a guilt trip on someone better than Maxi. The sisters looked embarrassed and couldn't meet our eyes, confirming Maxi's accusation. I placed my card on the coffee table. "If you change your minds and remember something, please give me a call."

We walked to our cars. "Why is everybody lying or not saying anything? It's not as if we were the cops or if we had proof of any wrongdoing."

"They're either afraid or ashamed. Or both," Maxi said.

"Ashamed I can understand, but afraid? Of whom and of what?"

"If we knew that, we'd have a strong clue to whoever killed Shirley and her son."

We parted. Maxi drove to her farm and I back to the agency.

At the office, I ate the soup Maxi had brought me. Then I wrote up my visit with the Washington sisters and placed it on Uncle Barney's desk. What to do next? The results of the adoption databases hadn't come in yet. It was too soon to bug my cousin Sam, a police lieutenant in the Westport

P.D., for anything he might have heard from the sheriff's office. Besides, he was always more forthcoming if I arrived with food, preferably something sweet. I'd have to do some baking after work.

My intercom buzzed. Lynn informed me that we had a new client and since Uncle Barney was out on a case, I would have to see him. I didn't mind, especially since the adoption case wasn't going anywhere. I took the prospective client into the conference room.

I didn't usually take an instant dislike to someone, but Merritt Barton might prove to be the exception. I'd been mentally undressed by men occasionally, but not in a business setting. What rankled worse was my suspicion that his conclusion was that he'd seen better.

Coolly I asked him what the agency could do for him.

"Run a check on someone."

I nodded and prepared to take notes. "Check on a job applicant?"

He steepled his fingers and smiled. "Not exactly. On a prospective mate."

"You are planning to get married?"

He snorted. "Not on your life. Four times was enough. What I pay in alimony could feed the population of a small country." He shuddered theatrically. "My son is talking about getting married. I want to know everything about the young woman."

I so didn't want to do this even though premarital investigations were becoming more and more the norm.

"What were you thinking of in terms of investigating?"

"I want to know if she's a gold digger out to entrap my son."

Now I was even less eager to take this case. "Are you saying you think your son isn't lovable for himself?" The moment the words had left my mouth, I knew I shouldn't have uttered them. Fully expecting Merritt Barton to leave the agency in a huff, he surprised me by chuckling.

"You obviously haven't met Perry. He's got it all: looks, charm, and money."

What about intelligence, sensitivity, compassion, morals? Naturally I didn't wonder about that out loud. "I'll need more information."

He handed me a sheet with the pertinent facts about his son. "And information on the young woman."

"Her name is Annette Ferris. Here's her address."

I took the piece of paper he held out to me. "Does she have a job?"

The corners of his mouth turned down before he replied. "Yeah. She's just a dumb little school teacher in town."

I wanted to reach across the conference table and yank out his tonsils. As calmly as I could, I said, "One, if she's a teacher, she most certainly isn't dumb. Two, the word *just* is totally out of place when talking about teachers. I suspect that neither one of us would last a day in a classroom." I stood. "I don't think we're the right agency for this job."

"Now hold on a minute. You came highly recommended."

He was waiting for me to apologize. I didn't, though I

shuddered to think what Uncle Barney would have to say about this.

"Okay, okay. I'm sorry about what I said about teachers. I didn't mean it. I'd have said something like that about any woman in any profession who was after my boy."

"So all women only want your son's money?"

"And mine. I know that from experience, so I don't want him to marry a poor girl."

From his expression I knew that he was convinced of this and no argument could change his mind, even if I'd cared enough to try to change it. And I still wanted to turn down the case, but business was a little slow. I only had the MacNiall case. I pressed the button on the phone to summon Lynn and the necessary forms.

When he had completed them and had given Lynn a retainer, we watched him leave. Standing next to me, Lynn made that hissing sound which always made me think of a big snake.

"I don't like that man," she said.

"For once we agree on something."

"He is bad. Evil, black aura all around him," she said, shuddered, and hurried back to her desk as if to get away from this aura as fast as possible.

I didn't know anything about auras, evil or otherwise, but I didn't want to spend time with Merritt Barton if I could help it. Still, his retainer would help pay my salary.

"What did he list as his occupation?" I asked.

There was a pause while she looked for the information. "President of Barton Industries," Lynn said, clearly impressed. "Big factory east of town. Make parts for machines. We could have charged him more."

I ignored the last statement. She couldn't seem to grasp the idea that if we charged more, we wouldn't have the repeat clients we had. Nor would we be recommended so frequently to prospective clients.

Consulting my directory of Westport Community Schools, I found that Annette Ferris taught fifth grade at the Samuel Adams Elementary School, one of the oldest schools in town. Since the school was only a few blocks from the agency, I thought I might be in time to catch a glimpse of Annette.

Dismissal time was probably the most chaotic time of the school day. The main door was unlocked and nobody challenged me in the hallway. On a bulletin board near the office, the teachers' names and room numbers were listed. I followed the arrow to Room 102, Annette's room.

The kids were lining up outside her door under her calm direction. She was an attractive mid-twenties woman, light-brown highlighted hair, blue eyes, slender. Perry Barton had good taste. I just hoped he was nicer than his father. I returned to my car, which I'd parked in the teachers' parking lot.

Half an hour later Annette came out, carrying a bunch of folders. Homework to be graded? I followed her, hoping she was going straight home. She was.

The Stratford Arms Apartments were not nearly as elegant as their name suggested. I guessed them to be one-bedroom flats, laid out in shotgun fashion.

Now I knew what she looked like and where she lived. I could have left, but something made me linger. A few minutes later, a white Lexus parked in front of the building. The young man going into the building was probably Perry Barton. He had his father's dark hair and he certainly was good-looking. I copied his license plate number. Time to go home and bake something delicious enough to get my cop cousin, Sam, to run the license plate through the system to establish his identity.

Luke was right. It had been madness on my part to buy such a large, old house. Still, if I had to do it over I'd choose it again. My heating bills were astronomical and yet the house was never truly warm. I was learning the value of layering my clothes. I had even closed most of the upstairs heating registers and used the downstairs library as my bedroom. I rather liked having my bed in the middle of the room, surrounded by bookcases against all the walls.

The coolness of the house was also why I didn't mind baking. Not only did baking make my kitchen fragrant but toasty warm as well. Buddy sat a few feet away, waiting for dough crumbs to fall to the floor.

"Cats aren't supposed to like cookie dough," I told her. "It doesn't taste like tuna." To prove my point, I pinched off a tiny piece and gave it to her. She practically inhaled it and looked at me, waiting for more.

"You're weird, but I know why you like the dough. It's all that sweet butter in it. If you don't watch out, Buddy, you're going to look like a butterball."

After I put the cookies into the oven, I phoned Sam. He was working the five to midnight shift. I offered him a trade: cookies for the name of the owner of the Lexus. He was willing to trade and told me to come to the office.

Knowing that Sam probably hadn't eaten dinner yet and that, given the current understaffing of the Westport P.D., he might not have a chance to go out for a meal, I used the last of Maxi's homemade bread to make him a hefty sandwich.

Sam was on the phone when I arrived at his office, but he motioned me inside. I sat in the visitor's chair and held my two paper sacks on my lap.

Seeing them, he quickly ended the call. "What you got there, cuz?"

"A turkey sandwich on Maxi's bread with just a touch of horseradish mayo and your favorite butter cookies." I watched his face light up.

"Glory be," he said reverentially. Then he handed me a piece of paper. "The Lexus is registered to Barton Industries."

"To the company? I've seen utility vehicles registered to a company but a luxury car?"

Sam shrugged. "I'm no tax expert, but it's gotta have something to do with tax benefits."

"What do you know about Barton Industries?"

"Probably not more than you do. Their plant is surrounded by a high wall. The gate is guarded by a guy who looks like he knows how to use the gun strapped around his middle. Whatever it is they make, they get government contracts from time to time. At least according to our newspaper."

"The government gives contracts for all sorts of things. Some even benign," I mused. We sat in silence while Sam ate his sandwich with obvious gusto.

"Anything you can pass on from the sheriff about Shirley's and Rodney's murder?"

"What in particular are you interested in?" Sam asked.

"Their finances. Both Uncle Barney and I think they lived above their means."

Sam quirked an eyebrow at me. "Isn't that pretty much the American way? Buy now and no payment until next year. Or buy two and get one free. And then there's the layaway plan, etc. etc."

"That assessment is a little harsh," I said, though there was a lot of truth to it.

"There's a combined city-county law enforcement seminar next week. I'll ask the sheriff about the Dwyer case. If he asks why I'm interested, I'll tell him my nosy cousin is the one who found the bodies. Too bad you can't give him any cookies or sandwiches."

"And why can't I?"

"It could be seen as a bribe."

"And with you this isn't a bribe . . . because?"

"Because we're family, taking care of each other."

"Uh-huh." I told him good-bye and left.

In the parking lot I sat in my car for a minute, thinking. I needed to get into Shirley's house and do some serious snooping. Few people threw away everything. If she had been blackmailing someone, there just might be some evidence.

Though it was only six o'clock, night had fallen. I couldn't leave my car in the Dwyer's driveway for anyone to see. If I hid it where I'd sat during surveillance, I'd have a long slog through deep snow in the dark. That didn't sound appealing at all. Better wait until morning.

Thank heaven it hadn't snowed again. All the country roads were clear. Not only was that great for safe driving, but I wouldn't leave a fresh set of tire prints at the Dwyer house for the sheriff to wonder about.

I parked the Jeep behind the trees and walked to the house. From talking with Sam I knew that the blood had been cleaned up and the room disinfected. Still, I dreaded entering the house. Telling myself not to be such a wimp, I wondered where I should look first for the spare key most people hid outside: near the front entrance or the back door? I didn't find it by the front door. Careful to step into the footprints made by the police, I circled to the back. There I found it taped to the underside of a wooden planter that contained the dead stalks of last summer's flowers.

The kitchen had that airless smell common to locked up rooms accompanied by faint traces of the disinfectant used in the living room. I saw the dogs' food bowls and wondered how they were doing. They had been much doted on and had to miss their owners.

My search of the kitchen yielded nothing but the realization that the Dwyers must have lived on prepackaged food. The house was sparsely furnished, probably to allow Shirley's wheelchair easy passage through the rooms. Whatever the reason, I was grateful as it made my search easier.

I found nothing of interest until I took a closer look at Shirley's antique four-poster bed. One of the posts leaned a little to the right. Could posts be unscrewed? I investigated and found that this one did. In the hollowed out part I found a roll of papers. Carefully I eased them out. Before I had a chance to look at them, I heard a car approach.

Risking a quick look out the window, I saw a black Lincoln ease into the driveway. My heart jumped into my throat. The house offered no good hiding places so I ran out the back door and stopped. My footprints would be a dead giveaway unless I stepped into the prints made by the police officers, except those led only to the front of the house. No good.

Frantically I looked around. Slipping under the porch seemed to be the only hiding place. I stuffed the papers into my coat pocket and got down on my hands and knees, praying that snakes and other creepy crawly things had remembered that they were supposed to hibernate. Once I was under the porch, I saw that I had left a few footprints pointing to my location. I crawled back out and, moving backward, I smoothed them out just in time to hear the back door being opened.

I held my breath, hoping I wouldn't have to sneeze or cough. I even tried to quiet my labored breathing. The footsteps were heavy, suggesting that a man stood above me. The chauffeur? Francis MacNiall? He seemed to stand there for a long time. Finally, he went back inside.

I heard movement in the house. More than one person, from the sounds. Were they looking for the papers I had discovered only minutes earlier? What was in them to risk breaking and entering? Except I hadn't heard anything being broken or forced open. They'd had a key. How had they come by it? Had there been a second hidden key?

Lying on the frozen ground, I shivered violently and wondered how long it took for a body to freeze to death. I glanced at my watch every few minutes. A full fifteen minutes later, I heard the car start and drive away. I crawled from my hiding place. I was so cold that I moved like a zombie. It seemed to take forever for me to reach my car. I sat in it, waiting for it to warm up a little before I drove to my grandmother's house.

Maxi made a pot of Earl Grey tea which she sweetened with honey. She also made me buttered toast sprinkled with cinnamon and sugar, a childhood favorite.

After I had thawed out, we looked at the papers I'd found. The top one was a birth certificate for a baby girl named Chelsea. Where it asked for the father's name, it said "unknown." The second sheet was identical to the first except the baby was unnamed.

"Why is there no name?" I wondered.

"Maybe it was easier to give her away if she was nameless," Maxi said.

"But they gave Chelsea away and she had a name."

"Maybe the other baby died."

"Wouldn't there have to be a death certificate?"

"Under normal circumstances yes, but these are hardly normal conditions," Maxi said.

"And the father is unknown?" I shook my head. "Liza knows who the father of her baby is. Or babies."

"She must have wanted to protect him."

I frowned. "Why? He got her pregnant. She was seventeen and her family wasn't supportive."

"We need to talk to her," Maxi said.

I shook my head again. "It'll be difficult to get her to talk to me. If I'm not alone, she'll probably say nothing."

"Then you go and let me know what she says."

I thanked Maxi for the tea and drove to Liza's place of business.

Chapter Five

I waited outside the clinic, hoping Liza would go to lunch at twelve. She did. I joined her on the sidewalk.

"Speak of the bad penny," she said with a grin.

"How are you?"

"How is anybody in midwinter in northern Indiana? Why anybody ever settled in this frozen hell hole when we have warm beaches in this country, I'll never understand."

"We do have lovely springs, summers, and autumns," I pointed out, "though right now they're hard to remember. Where do you usually eat lunch?"

"At Dirty Joe's."

"I don't believe I've heard of this establishment."

"That's my nickname for Joe's Eats," she said.

"How about we go to the Green Plate? My treat."

"That's that vegetarian place, right?"

"They also make great grilled cheese sandwiches and out of this world fruit smoothies."

"I bet they don't serve beer, do they?"

"I don't think so."

"It's Joe's for me."

If I wanted to talk to her, I had no choice but to follow Liza. She looked at me.

"You think I'm a bad person because I smoke and drink beer at lunch—"

"No, not at all. But I don't think you're happy. Depressed maybe? Have you been to a doctor recently?"

"No."

Her tone told me that she didn't want to talk about this with me.

We arrived at Joe's, which was so smoke-filled and dark that it was difficult to see if the word *dirty* was warranted. Probably was.

We took our coats off and sat at the bar.

"Hi, Joe," Liza greeted the cook we could see through the order window. Joe winked at her.

A waitress with big hair, who looked as if she'd be at home in a seventies sitcom, plopped two water glasses in front of us and asked Liza, "The usual?"

"Yeah. No, wait. Let me have a Chicago dog, hold the onions, and a brewsky."

Though I liked hot dogs, I wasn't brave enough to have one at Joe's, so I ordered a grilled cheese sandwich and a pot of tea.

"Any news?" Liza asked.

"Nothing conclusive. Tell me again what you remember about the night of the delivery."

Liza grimaced. "I remember pain. Awful pain. Somebody giving me something for it. The pain went on for hours. I remember being told to push. I heard a baby cry. There was more pain, more pushing. I heard a baby crying. They gave me something to drink, and I fell asleep. I told you all this before."

"Did you hear two babies cry or the same baby cry twice?"

"I've thought about that a lot," Liza said. "If it didn't sound so crazy, I'd say it was two different babies crying. But that would mean I'd given birth to twins. Surely they'd have told me."

"The way they told you about Chelsea?"

"Oh, no." Liza buried her face in her hands.

"When you went for your prenatal checkups, didn't the doctor tell you he heard two heartbeats?"

"What prenatal checkups? I told you I was a virtual prisoner for most of my pregnancy."

I stared at her, too shocked to say anything for several seconds. "Your mother and Miss Patricia ought to be locked up for criminal negligence."

"Too late for grandma. She's probably atoning for her sins down there." Liza pointed to the floor. "At least I hope so. She's got a lot to atone for. And Mom? She gets away with whatever she wants."

"Not this time." I considered how best to formulate my next question and decided it was best to ask it straight out. "What about the babies' father? How much did he know?"

"Just that I was pregnant."

"He didn't stand by you? Help you?"

"He couldn't. He was a married man with a family. Happily married, he claimed."

Not so happily married that he couldn't resist fooling around with a teenager and getting her pregnant, the scum.

"Though now I wonder about the happy marriage since he's been divorced and remarried a couple of times since then."

"Do you see him sometimes?"

"Occasionally."

"And?"

"And nothing. We pretend we know each other casually. Enough to say hello. His current wife is the one with the money, and she's extremely possessive and jealous." When Liza saw my expression, she added, "He's really not such a bad guy."

Yeah, right. "How much older than you was he?"

She shrugged. "Twenty years, maybe."

I so wanted to tell Liza what I thought of a middle-aged man who seduced a young girl, got her pregnant, and abandoned her, but I bit my tongue. "In all the years, your mother never let slip anything about who adopted the babies?"

"No, but Grandma once did. She said something like Chelsea would be taken care of. She'd even get her immunizations cheaply because her new family was in the business."

"In the business? That narrows it down to physicians, pharmacists, and men connected to pharmaceutical companies."

"Doesn't help much, huh?"

"On the contrary. Rules out people in a lot of professions, so we have fewer to look at. What did your mother reply to Miss Patricia's statement?"

"Something really weird. Something like if only the other little bastard had been that lucky." Liza stared at me, comprehension dawning. "At the time this didn't mean anything to me, or I didn't care what they said, but now it means that there really was another baby."

She picked up her beer mug, but it was empty. I signaled to the waitress. "Would you bring my friend a tall orange juice, please?" Liza looked so stunned that I figured she needed the benefits of the vitamins.

The food came, but Liza ignored her hot dog. I'd gotten fries with my sandwich. I kept putting them on her plate. Absentmindedly, she ate them. She needed food to counteract the shock. Eventually I persuaded her to eat her hot dog. By the time she lit her after-lunch cigarette, she seemed to have recovered somewhat.

"Will you please look for my babies?" she pleaded.

"Of course, but we have so little to go on. I really, really need to know the name of their father. It'll remain confidential if at all possible. Please, Liza. You don't have to protect him any longer."

She thought about this for a long time, occasionally taking a drag from her cigarette. "You're right. No reason to protect him any longer. Merritt Barton."

I almost fell off the bar stool. "Did you say Merritt Barton?"

"Yeah. Do you know him?"

I nodded. "He's a client, but on another matter."

She chuckled mirthlessly. "Small world, huh?"

I just sat there, stunned. What were the odds of two un-related cases crossing? Except Westport wasn't a large city, so unless you were a hermit, sooner or later you'd cross everyone's path. The same seemed to be true of cases.

"How did you meet him? You were what? Sixteen?"

"Yeah. He came to the house on business. Grandma liked to work from her home office. He was a good-looking man, and he paid attention to me. Just about the only adult in that mausoleum of a mansion who did. He said he loved me, and that's how it started."

"I can see how the attention of an older man would have been flattering to a neglected young girl."

"That's all it took to mess up my life," she said and smiled a little.

It was the kind of smile that threatened to bring tears to my eyes. I fiddled with the lid on the teapot to gain con-trol. "Did you tell him you were pregnant?"

"Yes. I met him one last time at our usual place, the potting shed. The gardener came only in the mornings, so we had the hothouse and the shed to ourselves."

"What did he say when you told him?"

"He was furious. Demanded to know why I hadn't been more careful. There was nothing he could do. He was married, and his wife would never divorce him."

"That's it?"

"He said he could scrape up some money. Not a lot because his wife was tightfisted."

Anger left me momentarily speechless. I drummed my fisted hands on the countertop.

"You're upset," Liza said.

"You think? If I had a sixteen-year-old daughter and some middle-aged Lothario left her pregnant, I think I'd tear out his liver and feed it to those big, black, raucous birds."

"That's why I didn't tell anyone about him."

"I don't understand that. Why protect him?"

"Because I loved him, and because he was going to give me money so the baby and I could get away from my family."

I hadn't met Miss Patricia but by all accounts she was even more unpleasant and dictatorial than Rose. "I would have wanted to get away too." I thought for a moment. "The reading of the will is next Monday?"

"At five in the lawyer's office."

"I'll wait outside the apartment for you."

"Why don't we just meet here. I'm sure I could use a drink afterward."

"Okay, I'll be here."

"I hope the old man left me enough so I can help my babies when you find them."

"Except they're not babies anymore," I pointed out.

"No, they aren't. They'll be ready for college. Maybe I could help out with tuition."

"That would be good." I left Liza there and went to the office, praying we'd find her daughters.

The fish fry was in full swing when I arrived at the church's fellowship hall. I bought three carryout platters from Maxi, who had saved three slices of her apple pie for me.

Uncle Barney and Luke joined me at home. We sat around the kitchen table with huge helpings of fish, potato salad, and slaw.

"Why does fish from a fish fry taste so good?" Luke asked.

"Because it's deep fried, and anything deep fried tastes good," I said.

"Why did you have to tell me that? Now I'm picturing what this is doing to my arteries," he said.

"When was the last time you ate anything deep fried? I know you always order a plain baked potato when you eat out."

"True. So I can enjoy this."

"Everything in moderation. Isn't that what was written on the temple at Delphi?" Barney asked.

"It might have been 'Nothing to Excess,' " I said, "which is pretty much the same thing."

I made a pot of coffee. We were too full to eat the pie so I wrapped their pieces for them to take home.

Luke had the early morning shift at the hospital so he left.

Uncle Barney and I drank another cup of coffee. "So how was your meeting with Francis MacNiall?"

"Uninformative until he let one thing slip after his third martini."

"And what was that?"

"He said, 'Those girls have cost us plenty.' "

"Those girls? Plural. So there were two babies. If he was referring to them."

"I asked him if they paid the adoptive parents. He said no."

"Did someone blackmail them? The Dwyers? The attending physician?"

"Could be any one of them."

"Did he let anything else slip?"

"No."

"You think he knows where the girls are?"

"If anyone knows, it would be him. He strikes me as the sneaky type. The type who likes to hold things over people. Who glories in the fact that he knows something ´ no one else does."

"Doesn't sound as if you liked him."

"He isn't a likable human being. Maxi would probably describe him as being smarmy." When he saw my frown, he added, "Ask your grandmother what that means."

"I will." I paused, thinking. "Since his sister hired us to find Chelsea, he obviously hasn't told her."

"Miss Patricia was probably the prime mover in this

whole story. And she was extremely secretive. I suspect he found out somehow or she told him. Remember, Rose was only a MacNiall by marriage."

We talked for a few moments more before Uncle Barney left.

I crumbled the piece of fish I'd saved onto Buddy's plate and set it down. She ate it, breading and all. As I cleaned up, I thought about the case. How had Shirley gotten possession of the girls' birth certificates? And why had she kept them? What were the odds that she'd kept the adoptive parents' names somewhere as well? I knew I had to go back to her house. Of course, the chances that someone might see me increased with each visit, but that was a risk I had to take.

Since it was Saturday morning, I drove to the homeless shelter to help Maxi cook breakfast.

She was already in the kitchen, arranging frozen hash browns on cookie sheets.

I hugged her. "Are we serving sausage with the potatoes?"

"Yes. If you'll fry the patties, I'll butter the bread for the toast." She placed the potatoes into the oven. "Did you enjoy the fish?"

"Yes, and so did Luke and Uncle Barney and Buddy." I debated about confiding in her about my visit to Shirley's house.

"Why don't you just tell me or ask me whatever is bothering you?"

"Am I that transparent?"

"Only to me, Schatzi."

"I need to search Shirley's house again."

"Breaking and entering? Count me in."

"Oma, don't be so eager. I believe breaking and entering is a felony. Not that we'll break anything. I know where the spare key is."

"Clever girl. When will we break . . . um . . . visit her house?"

"As soon as possible. I'd planned on doing it after we serve breakfast."

"Hot diggety."

I couldn't help but smile at her. "You can be the look-out."

Two hours later we drove past Shirley's house. "That's the place," I told Maxi.

"Why aren't we stopping?"

"I want to be sure no one else is here."

"Ah. We're casing the joint."

I had to laugh. "Have you been reading whodunits or watching gangster movies on television?"

"Both."

"I thought you were into historical novels about the Boleyn sisters, Henry VIII, and Katharine of Aragon."

"Finished them. Now I'm in the mood for contemporary mayhem."

"For someone who appears so mild-mannered, you sure have a bloodthirsty streak in your reading material."

"Vicarious bloodthirstiness is allowed," she said piously.

I turned the car around and drove back to the house. "Why don't you stay in the car. If anyone pulls into the driveway honk the horn."

"Okay, but wouldn't it be faster if we both searched?"

"Yes, but how could I explain you being in the house if someone stopped and challenged us? This way I can stretch the truth a little and claim that I was hired."

"You were. Just not specifically to search the Dwyer house."

I left Maxi in the car. Keeping my gloves on, I unlocked the door and did a visual check. Shirley had spent her time in a wheelchair. How high or how low could she reach? I looked around the house until I found her wheelchair. Would it be macabre if I sat in the chair? Maybe, but it would allow me to search faster.

Maneuvering the wheelchair without bumping into the furniture was harder than I'd thought.

From a sitting position, the kitchen offered the most drawers and cupboards as hiding places. I found nothing that didn't belong in a kitchen until I got to the broom closet. There I found what looked like a broom handle, except it had a curious device on one end. Not knowing what it was, I took it to the car for Maxi to look at.

"Do you have any idea what this is?"

"I know exactly what it is. My friend, Irene, who is wheelchair bound, has one just like it. She uses it to change light bulbs on her ceiling lights."

"Thank you." As I turned away, she grabbed my arm.

"Maybe we should ask Irene to help us. She'd spot good hiding places someone in a wheelchair would use."

"Really, Oma. I'm not inveigling someone else into breaking the law. Especially not someone in a wheelchair."

"Irene would think this a hoot." Maxi sighed dramatically. "Why are the young never any fun?"

I just shot her a long-suffering look before dashing back into the house.

Both the dining room and the hall had chandelierlike light fixtures on the ceiling. Though I couldn't picture Shirley climbing onto the middle of the dining table to change a bulb, I couldn't take a chance and omit checking it. Taking my shoes off, I climbed up and checked the chandelier. There was nothing.

I could picture Shirley using the pole to change a bulb in the hall. I tried the pole several times unsuccessfully, so I searched the house until I found a stepladder in the pantry.

The hall fixture was modeled on a wagon wheel. I noticed that a couple of the spokes on the wheel were not as dusty as the rest. I unscrewed them and hit the jackpot. The spokes had been hollowed out. Using a pencil, I extracted a rolled up piece of paper from each. I replaced the spokes, put the stepladder back where I'd found it, and looked around carefully to see that everything was back where it had been. Then I beat a hasty retreat.

"That was fast," Maxi said when I rejoined her in the car.

I handed her the papers and backed out of the driveway.

"What do you make of these?" she asked after a cursory examination.

"Nothing yct. I want to get away from here before I look at them."

"Nobody's around. There's nothing to worry about."

"Not for you maybe because you'd slip into your dithery little old lady act and nobody would believe you'd ever do anything illegal. Me, they'd haul off to jail."

She chuckled. "Age has a few advantages. Not many, but some."

At Maxi's farm, she brewed a pot of coffee before we studied the slips of paper.

"We have letters of the alphabet and numbers," I murmured.

"Sums of money. Initials. Of people, I presume?"

"Locations and dates?" I thought for a moment. "If Shirley extorted money, where is it? I looked at last year's income tax return and tax statements. It all looked legitimate. She has a retirement fund and social security."

"With just that income, could she afford the upkeep and the taxes on this place? Not to mention the new SUV?" Maxi asked.

"Maybe. There's no mortgage on the place, and I assume that her son helped out." I thought for a moment. "If they were receiving regular blackmail payments, where is the money?"

"Don't some people have offshore bank accounts in the Caribbean?"

"Oma, I doubt that the Dwyers were sophisticated enough to know how to go about opening such an account. And if they did, there's no way we could get that kind of information. No, the money's got to be closer to home."

"You're right. A safety deposit box in a bank?"

"Maybe, but that's something the sheriff's department would have looked at immediately. We need to ask Sam."

Maxi got up and opened her refrigerator. She nodded, pleased. "I can whip up a meal and take it to him at five. You know he can't resist food."

"Especially your food. I'll meet you at the police station at five." I gathered up the pieces of paper and finished my coffee.

Maxi walked me to the door and hugged me.

Back at the office, I saw Glenn come out of Uncle Barney's office. "How's the surveillance of Miss Annette Ferris going?"

"Uneventful. She's just what she appears to be: a nice schoolteacher. She and her fiancé go to dinner, dancing, walks, the movies. All the sort of things young people do who are dating. Barney wants to see you."

I knocked on the door and entered.

"Cybil, I need you to take over surveillance of Miss Ferris tonight. Glenn has an emergency assignment."

"Okay, but I was going to join Oma when she takes food

to Sam and pumps him for information on the Dwyer's possibly having a safety deposit box."

"I think she can handle that little task all by herself."

I nodded. Oma could get information out of a broom handle. "When do I start surveillance?"

"Glenn reported Miss Ferris's return from shopping a half hour ago. This being a Saturday evening, she'll probably go out. Grab some food and go over there."

I nodded and left.

Since my house was only a few blocks from the agency, I drove home, petted Buddy, and fed her. Then I took a fast shower, changed into a dressier outfit of gray flannel slacks and matching jacket with a gray and black checked silk blouse, and boots with medium-high heels. Now I felt I could follow the young couple into a fancy restaurant if I had to. I fixed a sandwich and a thermos of coffee. In case I had to sit in a cold car for any length of time, I grabbed a blanket and went to my car.

I wasn't parked long in front of her apartment building when Perry Barton arrived in his Lexus. He parked and went in. A few minutes later he came out with Annette. I followed them. When they headed for the toll road, I groaned. What if they were off to a weekend in Chicago? I phoned Uncle Barney. He said to follow them to wherever they were going and call him back.

I was approaching the exit to the southern shore of Lake Michigan when it began to snow. I groaned again. This part of the state was notorious for having masses of lake-effect snow dumped on it. Fortunately, Perry took that exit and didn't continue to Chicago. But where was he going?

Ten minutes later I knew. Brightly illuminated billboards announced the gambling casino on the boat docked in the small harbor. I was praying that they came to eat dinner onboard and not to spend the whole evening gambling. When they hadn't come out two hours later, I knew my prayer hadn't been answered. I had no choice but to follow them.

I confess I do not understand the love of gambling. Why would anyone willingly throw their hard-earned money away? Everyone knows that the chances of winning are in favor of the house and, despite an occasional win, very few people ever recoup their losses.

With great misgivings I went onboard. I checked the crowded dining room. They were not there. The fragrance of good food made me long for something more than the plain cheese sandwich I'd eaten in my car. I set out to find Perry and Annette. I spotted him sitting at a poker table. Annette stood behind him. He was toying with a chip from the considerable stack in front of him.

I hid behind a slot machine from where I could watch them. Whenever an employee came near me, I grudgingly dropped a quarter into the machine. From what I observed, Perry wasn't a good poker player. He didn't seem to take nearly as long as the other players to study his cards and to bet. Annette's fingers plucked at the scarf around her neck. Several times she whispered into his ear, but he waved her away. Was she trying to get him to quit playing?

In an astonishingly short time, Perry had lost all his chips. He downed his third drink and stormed out of the casino.

I followed them to the parking lot. By the time I started to brush off the snow from my car, the Lexus tore past me, going much too fast. Even though I hurried, by the time I left the parking lot I'd lost sight of their car. Assuming that they were returning to Westport, I took the toll road east.

Less than ten minutes later I saw the tail lights of a car in the shallow ditch beside the highway. I knew it was the Lexus even before I stopped.

Chapter Six

"Is everyone okay?" I called out as I ran toward the Lexus. Both of them were leaning against the car. "Have you called nine-one-one?"

Annette answered. "We called a tow truck."

"What happened?"

"I drove too fast. Hit a patch of ice and landed us in the ditch," she said.

It was too dark to read her expression, but I could have sworn she avoided eye contact. I could also have sworn I saw her sitting in the passenger seat as they zipped past me in the parking lot. She must really love the man to take responsibility for an accident she hadn't caused. I wanted to tell her if he let her do this he wasn't worthy of her, but this really wasn't my business. If they didn't rush into marriage she, hopefully, would discover this truth for herself in time.

"If you're okay, I'll go on," I said.

"Thanks for stopping. That was nice of you," Annette said.

Perry had yet to say word one to me. I was fairly sure his expression was sulky. There were few things I disliked more than sulking. Especially in men.

By the time I got back to Westport, it was too late to report to Uncle Barney, so I drove home. My little orange tabby came running as soon as I unlocked the front door. It was nice not to come home to an empty house.

First thing the next morning I phoned Uncle Barney and reported to him before he left for Indianapolis.

"Merritt Barton is scheduled to come in today at ten for a preliminary report. Cybil, can you meet with him?"

I'd rather meet with a python but didn't say so. "Yes," I replied, hoping I didn't sound as unenthusiastic as I felt.

I dressed in my most severely professional-looking suit and went to the office. After writing my report of the previous day's events, I placed it in the case folder and went downstairs.

At least he was prompt. Without being asked, Lynn brought coffee. On a silver-plated tray yet.

"So, what did you find out about the . . . um . . . little school teacher?" he asked, leaning forward to take a sip of coffee.

"Only good things. Miss Ferris is well thought of by her fellow teachers, and the kids in her class like her." I was quoting verbatim from Glenn's report.

"Yeah, she does come across as sincere and nice."

"Maybe because that's what she actually is."

"Maybe, but I want to be sure."

"Okay. I witnessed something last night that might just be the proof you want." I paused, formulating how I was going to say this. "Did your son tell you that he was in a car accident last night?"

"Perry mentioned something about dinging up his Lexus a little."

"It was more than just a ding. He ended up in a ditch. He'd been to the casino where he lost at the tables. I saw him drink enough that he never should have been behind the wheel of a car. When I caught up with them, Miss Ferris claimed she had been driving. I'm sure it was your son who'd lost control of the car. Now why would a woman take responsibility for an accident she had nothing to do with? Seems to me she must love your son very much. She saved him from getting a DUI."

Merritt Barton squirmed a little in his chair. "Well, yeah. Still, I want you to dig a little deeper."

I suppressed a sigh of exasperation. "What is it you're really after? Miss Ferris is hardly old enough to have a deep, dark past."

"Age has nothing to do with it. She could have a juvenile record. Could have had a teenage pregnancy."

He kept talking but my mind couldn't get past the "teenage pregnancy." Because he'd gotten a teenaged girl pregnant he expected others to do the same?

"A teenage pregnancy," I said, staring hard and long at

him. He got up, tugged at his tie and said, "Check a little deeper before you send me your final bill. I've got to go. Another appointment."

Oh, we would send him a bill all right. I'd charge him for every second I'd worked on the case. Out of the courtesy Uncle Barney demanded from his staff, I walked him to the door.

Consulting my notebook, I calculated my time and wrote down the number. "Lynn, keep a record of the billable hours for Mr. Barton and the miles traveled so far. He wants us to stay on the case."

"Okey dokey."

Lynn really liked this part of her job.

On Monday I waited in the office until it was time for Liza to call me. I was dying to know the terms of her father's will. While I sat at my desk, I pulled out the photocopy I'd made of the bits of paper retrieved from Shirley Dwyer's wagon wheel chandelier.

CR 70 & DR   - 500.00 - (5 - 100) - 1st
CR 50 & MCR - 500.00 - (5 - 100) - 15th
CR 80 & KWR - 500.00 - (5 - 100) - 30th

The last column listed dates and the column in front of it probably money in amounts and denominations. Fifteen hundred tax-free dollars in a month was nothing to sneeze at. But what was the money for? Services rendered? Blackmail? And what did the other letters and numbers mean? I had no idea.

And where were the fifteen hundred dollars? I had

looked at the bank statements for both Shirley and Rodney. Neither account contained anywhere near this amount. If it was money they were paid for doing something illegal, they would have received it in cash.

Fifteen hundred in one hundred dollar bills wasn't a very thick stack and could easily be hidden. When I found the slips of paper in the hollowed-out wheel spoke, I'd quit searching. Now I'd have to go back. I didn't relish the idea. Sooner or later somebody was bound to see me and wonder what I was up to. It could even be the sheriff. A night in county jail until bail could be posted was nothing to look forward to. Nor were the subsequent legal troubles and a possible jail sentence.

My phone rang, distracting me from my contemplation of jail. The reading of the will ended earlier than expected. Liza was in a cab on her way to her favorite bar. Would I meet her there now? Of course, I would.

She was already ensconced on her usual bar stool, a half-empty martini glass in front of her. I was dying to know what had happened at the reading of the will but restrained myself long enough to order a diet Coke. I looked at her face but couldn't get a clue, except that she looked exhausted.

"So, what happened?"

She downed the rest of her cocktail and motioned to the bartender to fix her another. "Meeting my mom always calls for at least two martinis." She fished out the olives from her glass and ate them.

"Would you like something to eat?" I asked.

"No, thanks. I only eat these olives because they're soaked in gin. Otherwise I wouldn't touch them."

I waited quietly until her second martini arrived and she'd taken a sip. I leaned forward encouragingly. She lit a cigarette before she spoke.

"I'll be a little bit better off financially, but I won't get the bulk of my inheritance till I'm fifty. I'm sure Mom persuaded my father to do this. I guess she's hoping that by then I'll be mature enough to handle money." She grimaced. "Until then, I'll get the interest on the money each month. I could survive on that amount, but just barely, so I'll keep my job until I'm half a century old." Liza shrugged. "Chelsea, on the other hand, made out like a bandit. Or she will once you find her."

"That might be the reason your mother hired us."

"I'm sure it is. Chelsea inherited a big block of company shares. If Mom can manipulate her to vote her way, and Mom is a world-class manipulator, she'll have controlling interest in the company."

"What's the setup now?"

"She and Uncle Francis own an equal amount of shares, so the company's run by compromise and consensus which doesn't sit well with Mom. She likes to be the queen bee and have complete control over everything around her."

I was beginning to think that finding Chelsea might not be a good thing, but we had accepted the job and I didn't think Uncle Barney would agree to dropping the case.

"What's bothering you?" Liza asked. "Having second thoughts about finding Chelsea?"

I shrugged.

"Don't forget that I'm her mother. Don't judges usually grant custody to the mother?"

"Usually, but her adoptive parents may not agree to give her up," I said.

"They didn't adopt her legally. I may not remember everything from that night, but I'm sure I didn't sign any papers. I never agreed to give up my baby. Or babies. They were stolen from me."

"If there were two babies, why is only one mentioned in the will?" I hated to ask this question, but I felt I had to prepare Liza for the grim possibility it suggested.

Her eyes widened. She drained her glass before she spoke. "You think my other baby didn't make it?"

"I don't know." I forced myself to maintain eye contact.

Tears filled her eyes but she nodded. "If she'd survived, it wouldn't make sense to try to find only one of my girls. Or leave all that money only to Chelsea. This is such a nightmare. Right now I could gladly strangle my mother."

I understood her anger and her pain. I sat quietly beside her.

"You will keep on looking?"

"Yes."

"And you will keep me informed?" she pleaded.

"Officially I can't since you're not our client, but I'll find a way to let you know when I find your daughter."

"That's all I ask."

"I better get back to work," I said. I hated to leave her sitting there, but the sooner I found her daughter, the sooner Liza would feel better. At least I hoped that's what would happen.

I had just reached my car when my cell phone chimed. It was Maxi.

"Can you come to the farm for dinner? I'm fixing chicken and dumplings."

Her dish wasn't the pale, starchy common variety, but the Austro-Hungarian version, redolent with sweet paprika. I wasn't about to refuse this tempting offer. "When?" I asked with shameless eagerness.

"As soon as you can get here."

"I'm on my way."

I took the bypass which formed a circle around Westport and so missed most of the early-evening traffic. I reached the farm in time to watch Maxi drop the dumplings into boiling broth with a soup spoon.

How she could get them to come out all the same size baffled me. Mine always turned out in all sizes and shapes known to mankind. When the dumplings rose to the surface, Maxi drained them and added them to the chicken. She served a Bibb lettuce salad dressed with olive oil and red wine vinegar.

Maxi let me eat silently until I'd stilled my hunger. "This has to be my all-time favorite dish," I said, sighing happily.

Maxi smiled. "I thought it was apfelstrudel."

"That's my favorite dessert."

"Funny, both you and Luke like the same dishes," she

said. "And speaking of Luke, I made enough to feed him as well. Will you take it to his apartment?"

I glanced at her suspiciously, wondering if she was matchmaking again, but her gaze when it met mine was innocent of guile. She liked Luke enough to want to treat him to his favorite foods.

"Speaking of feeding men, did you talk to Sam yet?"

"Yes. Over his favorite beef stew and hot rolls he talked about the Dwyer case. Seems the sheriff had the house searched for any and all possible clues to the murder and found nothing suspicious. That includes large amounts of cash. And no trace of a safety deposit box key."

"When did he search the house?"

"Right after the bodies were removed."

"Before I searched and found those pieces of paper."

"Seems to me they didn't search as thoroughly as you did. He did tell Sam one interesting thing. They found a few drops of blood by the front door that doesn't match the victims' type."

It took a second before the significance of this hit me. "It has to belong to the murderer. Rodney must have fought back and injured his attacker." I sighed. "This doesn't help us until we have a strong suspect."

"True, but we need to go back for another look." Maxi held up her hand before I could speak. "I'll be the lookout again."

"Did you notice that shed not far from the house?"

"Yes."

"It doesn't seem like a secure area to stash cash," I said.

"No, but the money could be hidden behind some loose boards, up in the rafters, or buried under the floor. I say we go back there tomorrow morning."

"I hate to park the car by the house again. One of these times someone will become suspicious."

"We can come up with a reasonable explanation," Maxi said.

"Such as?"

"I could be out walking Hiram," she said.

"Oma, that small dog will sink up to his pointy little ears in the snow."

"I'll only use him as an excuse if anyone stops. Or better yet, I could say that the property was coming up for sale, which it is, and I was interested in buying it."

I shot her a disbelieving look.

"Why not? I already own a farm. It's not illogical for me to want more land."

I had to admit that this might work. Maxi fixed containers of food for Luke and Sam and sent me to deliver them. I promised to be back at the farm by seven-thirty the next morning.

Luke's place being closer, it was logical for me to drive there first. If he wasn't in, I'd leave the food with the apartment manager, a dedicated hypochondriac who loved having a sympathetic physician as a tenant. Part of me hoped that Luke wouldn't be home. Part of me wanted to see him.

Music from behind his door told me that he was home. Odd that it wasn't the usual classical music he listened to but a popular top-forty radio program. And he didn't usually play music at this volume. I knocked twice before he heard me and opened the door.

"Cybil, what brings you here?" he asked with a smile.

"Oma sent—" And that's when I saw her, sitting in one of the easy chairs, her white uniform short enough to be rucked up above her knees. I thought nurses had to dress more conservatively than that. I became uncomfortably aware that I was wearing my old parka and that I'd wrapped a knitted scarf around my hair. I probably looked like an old, bedraggled baba from the Russian steppes. Pulling myself together, I said, "Oma sent food."

"Great. I can tell from the aroma that it's one of my favorites."

"She said to refrigerate it for tomorrow." Then in a low voice, I added, "It's only one serving." There was no way on earth I'd allow his female company to enjoy Oma's food. I flicked another look at the woman.

"Oh, Cybil, that's Debbie Johnson. She works at one of the clinics. The nurses are planning a fund-raiser. Debbie meet Cybil."

"Cybil Quindt," I said, with emphasis on my last name.

"Nice to meet you," she said in a high, girlish voice.

I muttered a nice-to-meet-you back which was a big, fat lie. I didn't know whether I'd rather heave the dish of food at her or turn around and leave. Luke made the decision for me by taking the casserole from my hands. I didn't exactly run, but I didn't linger either.

I didn't remember driving to the police station until I forcefully plunked down the other casserole on Sam's desk. He scooted his chair back, blinking at me in alarm.

"Oma sent food," I said grimly.

"So I see and I appreciate it, but who're you mad at? What's wrong?"

"Why should anything be wrong?"

"Because you rush in here and dump the dish on my desk so hard I'm surprised it didn't break, and you're spitting mad. That's not like you. What happened?"

"Luke," I said, took a jittery breath and collapsed onto the nearest chair.

"Luke? What about him?"

"He's entertaining some bleached blond who works in one of the clinics, that's what."

"Well, from what I've observed, you're not entertaining him, so—"

"I know, I know. Me feeling this way makes no sense." I heaved a deep sigh. "I don't know why it bothered me so to see that woman in his apartment."

"Maybe because you still care a lot about Luke?"

"Of course I care about him. He's still my husband." I gnawed on my lower lip. "What upsets me is that I didn't think he'd—" My voice trailed off as I identified this irrational emotion that gripped me. I was jealous—plain and simple. Then a surge of anger hit me. "You don't see me entertaining peroxide blond hunky orderlies, do you?"

"I can't imagine you entertaining any hunks."

"And what do you mean by that? I'm not young or pretty enough?"

"No, no," he added hastily. "Just that you've always preferred the intellectual types over the hunks."

I took a couple of breaths, trying to calm myself. I paced in front of his desk. "What is it with men and bleached blondes?"

Sam shrugged.

"From Marilyn Monroe to Madonna—" I shook my head.

"As I said, why not consider entertaining him yourself? You obviously still care—"

"Or get a bleached blond hunk of my own," I said and headed for the door.

"Cybil, don't do anything rash!" Sam called after me, his voice alarmed.

"Eat your food," I said over my shoulder as I rushed out.

Not that there was much chance of my acquiring a hunk, blond or otherwise. I'd been with Luke so long that the idea of another man seemed preposterous. Obviously, men didn't have the same ethical qualms. Thinking about Luke and that woman caused me to make an illegal U-turn and head for the Y. A's cold pool and swimming laps till exhaustion set in seemed to be just what I needed.

Seven-thirty the next morning found me shivering in Maxi's driveway. She opened the rear door of my Volvo for Hiram to hop in before she joined me in the front. She placed two travel mugs in the car's holders. The coffee smelled great.

After murmuring a quiet good morning, I was silent. Although I was not usually a chatterbox, Maxi could tell something wasn't right. I knew she was flicking me those inquiring sideways looks.

"Want to tell me what's wrong now or after our mission is completed?"

"I'm not sure I'm going to tell you at all, but if I do it'll have to be after."

"Fair enough," she said and leaned back in her seat.

I couldn't believe she'd given up that easily. Was she ill? Now it was my turn to steal assessing looks at her.

"Cybil, I'd feel safer if you kept your eyes on the road. There are still treacherous patches of ice. Black ice."

She was right, as usual. It wouldn't be fully daylight for another fifteen minutes or so. I slowed our speed down to twenty miles an hour and kept my eyes on the road. The school buses had already collected the children, and people going to work were traveling in the opposite direction. I wasn't slowing anyone down.

Pulling into the Dwyer's driveway, I said, "Oma, please stay in the car. If anyone stops to question you, just say you're interested in the property and sent me to look at the outbuildings. Okay?"

"Okay." She opened her capacious bag and took out her knitting.

"You've started something new?"

She nodded. "For our Easter sale at church. The proceeds will go to the homeless shelter. You know that if I don't keep my hands busy, I nod off in front of the television and ruin a good night's sleep."

"Please lock the car doors behind me and don't get out for anyone." I swear Maxi was tempted to roll her eyes just then, but contented herself with a telling look. "If this takes a while, run the engine to keep warm."

Grabbing a flashlight, I headed for the shed. The snow was deep, yet I was sure that there were traces of footprints. Someone had come this way before the last big snowfall. The cops? Most likely. They might not have searched the house as thoroughly as I had, but they would have at least taken a quick look inside the shed. Or it could have been whoever was in the MacNiall car the day I'd hidden under the back porch. The memory of those moments made my heartbeat accelerate.

There was no lock on the door, but it was barred with a sturdy piece of wood that looked like a long ax handle. I slipped it from the metal brackets screwed to each door post. Now I faced the snow that had accumulated against the door. I should have brought a shovel. Rather than trudge back to the car, I used my booted feet to kick enough snow aside to open the door wide enough to slide through it sideways.

My powerful flashlight sliced through the dim interior, which was filled with stuff: two cardboard boxes, a vacuum cleaner, a wheelbarrow, flowerpots, a spade, a rake, some tools I didn't recognize, an old lawnmower, car tires, and a saddle. It would take hours to search through all this. I didn't want to spend that much time in the cold shed, so I decided to take the cardboard boxes with me to the car for a quick examination.

When Maxi saw me approach, she opened the door to the back seat. I placed the cartons next to Hiram, who sniffed them enthusiastically.

"I have no clue if there's anything in these which will help us. That shed is so full of stuff, it'll take hours to search through it."

"You want to look at the cartons at my house?"

"We better not add theft to our other transgressions," I said. "Let's go through the boxes now. You take one and I'll take the other, and then we'll trade."

"What are we looking for?" Maxi asked.

"I wish I knew."

"We'll recognize it when we see it?" she asked.

"I hope so," I said, remembering that I hadn't deciphered those pieces of paper from the chandelier.

For a while the only sounds in the car were the rustling of papers and the shifting of objects.

"What are you finding?" I asked.

"Mostly patterns and instructions for how to make quilts, how to embroider, knit, and crochet. What's in your box?"

"Receipts. Paid bills. Most of them dated last fall. Except . . ." I stared at the piece of paper in my hand.

"What is it?"

"A receipt from a hardware store for a carton of glass canning jars."

"What's so unusual about that? Some people still put up their own canned goods. I did until a couple of years ago. As I remember, you really liked my canned peaches," Maxi said.

"They were excellent. You'll have to teach me how to preserve fruit." I thought for a moment. "Where and at what time of year did you buy your jars and other canning stuff?"

"I got mine in a hardware store, and I usually bought them in early summer, just before I needed them. Why?"

"Rodney bought the jars in January."

Maxi frowned. "I didn't think the stores carried them year-round. They're usually displayed in the seasonal section in late spring and early summer."

"Maybe they were on sale in January?"

Maxi shook her head. "They would have been on sale last fall, after the canning season ended. You know, in time to make room for the winter and Christmas items. The Dwyers must have ordered them. When you searched the kitchen, did you see any homemade canned foods?"

I closed my eyes, visualizing the contents of the cupboards. "No. Lots of commercially canned goods but not a single Mason jar. What do you suppose they used them for? And where are they?" We both thought for a while.

Maxi shrugged. "I have no idea."

"I don't either." I put the receipt aside and continued the search, but neither of us found anything else that struck us as unusual. I returned the boxes to the shed, careful to put them back exactly where I had found them.

We had just started back to Maxi's farm when she asked, "What kind of floor does that shed have?"

"Hard-packed dirt." I stopped the car. We looked at each other. "I think I better have a good look at that floor." Slowly I backed up and parked in the driveway again.

"I'm coming with you," Maxi said. She took a pencil flashlight from her bag and followed me to the shed.

"If you hold my flashlight, I'll move the stuff around so we can look at the floor underneath."

Half an hour later—and considerably dustier and dirtier—we conceded defeat.

"Nobody has dug up this dirt floor in years, if ever," I said, my voice deflated.

"Schatzi, it was a good idea to look. Through the ages people have buried all kinds of things," Maxi said, her voice consoling.

We sat in the car with the heater on full blast to warm up before heading back to Maxi's farm.

"If the Dwyers took in fifteen hundred tax-free dollars a month extra for . . . probably quite a while, where is the money?" I wondered out loud. "They lived above their means but not that much. There must be money some-where. And that could lead us to their killer."

Maxi nodded. "The old follow-the-money theory. You're probably right."

Just then a patrol car pulled in behind us.

"Oh, oh," Maxi murmured. "We're busted."

Chapter Seven

Rolling down my window I waited for the deputy to approach, praying he wasn't one of the sheriff's men who'd been here on the day I found the bodies.

"Are you ladies having car trouble?" he asked, touching the brim of his hat in greeting.

"No," I said.

"Are you lost?"

"Not really."

Maxi leaned forward so he could see her. "We came to look at the place, officer. It's up for sale." She pointed to the For Sale sign stuck in the front yard. "I heard it's coming on the market at a reasonable price."

"Where did you hear that?" he asked with a frown.

"At the Crossroads Store."

He snorted. "Ma'am, I wouldn't believe everything I heard in that place. Bunch of loafers sitting around the stove gossiping." He looked around. Then, leaning down to look at us, he said, his voice conspiratorial, "You know what happened here? A double murder."

"My goodness!" Maxi exclaimed. "So this is the place? I read about it in the paper."

Maxi's surprised expression seemed so genuine that if I hadn't known better, I would have believed her myself.

"I'm sure my wife wouldn't want to live in a house where there'd been murders."

"I'm mostly interested in the land," Maxi assured him. "I own a farm and could use additional acreage."

"Good farming country around here," he agreed with a nod. "Well, have a good day, ladies."

We said good-bye and watched him leave.

Maxi waited until the patrol car was out of sight before she spoke. "You don't suppose Rose MacNiall or whoever was here found the money that day you hid under the porch?"

"She could have, though I'd think she'd be more interested in finding whatever it was Shirley was blackmailing her for."

"What could that be? Something to do with her granddaughter, Chelsea?"

"That's what I've been assuming, but maybe that's not it. Wouldn't Shirley have been just as guilty as Rose if she'd facilitated the illegal adoption?"

"I'm no lawyer, but it would seem so."

We stared through the windshield at the wintry landscape. "I'm so tired of the cold," I said.

"In a month we'll see the first crocuses," Maxi assured me.

"I wonder if the ones I planted will come up."

"Why wouldn't they? Anyway, let's go to my place. I made cinnamon twists."

"You did?" The thought of those fragrant pastries and Maxi's excellent coffee cheered me up.

A half hour later, pleasantly full and warm in Maxi's homey kitchen, the world looked a lot better to me until she brought up my estranged husband.

"I made some twists for Luke too. Did he like the food you took to him last night?"

"I assume so. I didn't stay." I could feel Maxi's eyes studying me.

"Did you two have an argument?"

"No."

"But?"

"But he had company. A woman."

"There could be a number of innocent explanations."

"I doubt that."

"What did she look like?"

"Mid-twenties. Slender. Bleached-blond hair."

"Ah. And seeing her there bothered you?"

"Of course. Luke's still my husband."

"You might remember that more often."

"Sam suggested the same thing."

"Good advice." Maxi handed me the wrapped pastries. We hugged before I left.

It didn't occur to me that maybe the woman was still at his place until after I'd knocked on Luke's door. What was I going to do if that was the case? Die on the spot. I was bending down to leave the pastries by the door when I heard his sleepy voice.

"Who's there?"

"Me, Cybil. Maxi sent cinnamon twists. I'll just leave them out here."

"No! Someone might take them. As good as they smell, they're temptation personified."

I heard the chain being removed. A moment later I faced Luke. He wore his usual cold weather sleeping attire: flannel pajama bottoms and a tee shirt.

"Come on in. I just made coffee."

If the woman was still here, Luke wouldn't have asked me in. Suddenly the morning wasn't as wintry. On the way to his kitchen, I glanced into his bedroom. Only one side of the bed looked slept in. I felt like breaking into song. Then the absurdity of my reaction hit me. *What was wrong with me?* We lived apart at my insistence and yet another woman in Luke's life bothered me a lot. At some point I'd have to sort this out.

Luke's small kitchen faced east. "Look, Cybil, the sun is coming out."

And not just literally, I thought. "Oma reminded me that in a month's time, the crocuses will bloom."

He smiled. "She was always more in tune with nature's calendar than the paper version. Do you have time for a cup of coffee?"

"Yes," I said, even though I'd have to put up with Lynn's disapproving looks and comments when I arrived late at the agency.

Lynn, being predictable, didn't disappoint me.

"You are late again. Just because the boss isn't here doesn't mean we can . . . how do you say? Goof off?"

"You said we. I'm not goofing off. Does that mean you are?" I smiled at her before I prudently hightailed it into my office.

The report on birth certificates had arrived. I studied it. Seven girls had been issued birth certificates in the county courthouse on April 22, the birthday of Liza's daughters. While I was still staring at the computer printout, Maxi phoned.

"Any new developments?" she asked.

I told her about the birth certificates. "So I'll start looking for these seven girls. Or maybe only six, if one of Liza's baby girls died at birth. Except I won't know which one not to look for."

"And since all of this was hush hush, you probably won't find a regular birth certificate for Chelsea," Maxi pointed out.

"Don't children need a birth certificate when they start school?"

"Yes. My guess is whoever adopted her was given a forged document."

"Probably." I thought for a moment. "You know what? I need to pay the Washington sisters another visit."

"We do. Just tell me when."

We hadn't done so well as a team the first time, so I wondered if it wouldn't be better if I went alone. I could be scarier on my own. On the other hand, my grandmother had a moral authority that could be quite intimidating.

"Okay, but this time the gloves come off."

"Right. We won't accept any more lies. It would be easier if we had some tangible evidence to hold over them."

"True but we don't, so we'll have to bluff."

"When do you want to go?" Maxi asked.

"As soon as possible."

"I'll meet you at their house. It'll take me thirty minutes to get there."

"Park about a block away. We want the advantage of surprise."

Before leaving, I stopped in Glenn's office. He was scowling at a bunch of receipts on his desk.

"Making out your expense account?" I asked, suppressing a smile. Glenn, who got rattled by almost nothing, became unnerved by this simple task. But then Lynn always questioned some item and found fault with some part of his report.

"Whatever happened to just telling the secretary that I spent eight dollars for lunch and thirty-five for gas?"

"Lynn happened."

"Tell me about it," he muttered. "What can I do for you?"

"How would I go about getting a fake birth certificate locally?"

"And I'm the first person you ask about this? Am I some shady character who'd know this?"

"No, but you know some shady characters who'd have this information."

"That's true," he admitted with a grin. "You aren't in some kind of trouble?"

"Me? No, no. It's in connection with a case where the baby was born at home and everyone involved was sworn to secrecy and silence. Then the baby was illegally adopted."

"In our county?"

"Yes."

"Louie the Lug used to be a master forger."

"Louie the Lug? You're making this up."

"No, I'm not. Louie is a big guy. Really big. Hence his nickname. But he could do the most delicate and intricate forgeries with those huge hands of his."

"Would he be able to tell if a document was a forgery?"

"Probably. What kind of document?"

"A birth certificate. Where can I find him?"

"He retired a couple of years ago. Arthritis crippled his writing hand."

"This forgery was done years ago. And I really need to see him."

"He won't see you unless someone he trusts arranges it."

"Does he trust you?"

"Yes."

"Well?"

"I'll contact him. Might not happen until tomorrow, though."

"Thanks, Glenn."

"Did you find anything in the Dwyers' shed?"

"No. And I checked the dirt floor. It hadn't been dug up."

"What all was in the shed?"

I told him.

"A vacuum cleaner? I once found a stash of drugs valued at twenty thousand dollars in the dust bag. Did you check the bag?"

"No, I didn't." I felt like a clueless newbie.

"Might want to do that. It's a long shot, but you never know."

At this time of the day most people were at work, and parking on London Street wasn't a problem. I sat in my car until I saw Maxi park.

"The sisters are at home. Their car's in the driveway," I told Maxi, pointing to the white sedan. Together we walked up the porch. Again we knocked and waited.

"Letty? Jane Ann? I know you're in there. We won't leave until you open the door," Maxi said.

More silence.

"Well, would you rather talk to the police? I have a grandson on the force. He can arrange to have a couple of burly officers here in ten minutes or less."

Even though Maxi's voice didn't get strident, there was a steely edge to it. The door opened.

"Thank you, Letty. I'd just as soon not discuss aspects of your murky past where the whole street can hear. The statute of limitation does not run out on certain crimes."

Letty motioned for us to come in. "No need to accuse us of crimes," she said with an air of injured dignity.

Neither Letty nor her sister asked us to sit down, so we stood in front of the sofa on which Jane Ann reclined. On a little table beside the sofa rested the paraphernalia of the chronically ill. If I read the name on the vial correctly, Jane Ann was a diabetic.

"We only facilitated certain matters," Jane Ann said. "We placed unwanted babies with loving couples who wanted them."

"We're talking about a case where the baby was very much wanted by her mother," I said.

"Well, she was way too young—" Letty clapped a hand over her mouth. Jane Ann shot her an angry look.

"So, you know exactly the baby we're talking about. Her name was Chelsea. I don't know what her twin sister was named," I said.

"She wasn't—"

"Letty, shut up!"

"She wasn't named because?" Maxi asked. "Did she die of natural causes?"

"Mercy, yes. We never harmed a baby," Letty said, her voice high and thin.

"We only know what Shirley Dwyer told us," Jane Ann added.

"And that was?" I prompted.

"That she was going to have two newborn babies who needed a home."

"She said two?"

"Yes, when she first talked to us. Then when she came, she had only one baby. I asked her what happened to the other one. She said we didn't need to know."

"With whom did you place Chelsea?"

Both sisters remained mulishly silent.

"If you won't tell us, the cops will get it out of you. They have ways," I told them, my voice suggesting unspeakable horrors.

"You can't scare us," Letty said.

The phrase "the worm turns" shot through my mind. Why had I ever thought of Letty as weak? The look in her eyes suggested that if cornered, she could be a formidable opponent.

"I'm not trying to scare you. Just telling you how it is. The police can stall for quite a while before you can actually make your one phone call to your lawyer. If you have one. Jane Ann isn't well. How long do you think she could hold out?" I hated to threaten them but saw no other way to get the truth out of them.

"We have to speak with someone first," Jane Ann said. "Depending on what . . ."

"Depending on what he, she, they say? The Mac-Nialls?" I asked softly.

Jane Ann gasped, giving me the answer.

"We need a couple of days," Letty said.

"You have exactly forty-eight hours." With that I turned and left. Maxi stayed behind for a moment. When she caught up with me, I was kicking the front tire of my car.

"What's wrong?" she asked.

"I just love bullying little old ladies."

"Schatzi, you had no choice. They would only have lied to us again. They may still do so."

"I know. Did you stay behind to apologize for me?"

"Heavens, no! I told them that my granddaughter meant what she said. And that we'd be back in two days."

"Thank you for backing me up."

"I'll always back you up. Now I have to go to Mercy Shelter. We're expecting a donation of canned goods from a church group."

I didn't tell her that I was going to the Dwyer place. She would insist on coming, and she already had more than enough on her plate. She also looked pale. I didn't think being out in this cold weather was particularly good for her. Weren't the elderly susceptible to pneumonia? I would never forgive myself if she got sick because I let her help me on a case.

I checked for new tire and footprints in the Dwyer's driveway but didn't see any. Encouraged by this I left my car parked there and dashed toward the shed. I removed the wooden bar and slipped inside, closing the door behind me. A quick search of the vacuum cleaner and I'd be out of there.

It didn't go quite as fast as I'd thought. I had trouble opening the canister, as it was rusty and dented. Rummaging through a box of old tools, I found a screwdriver, which enabled me to pry the canister open. The paper bag didn't feel like stacks of money were hidden inside. Still, I emptied the contents onto a newspaper. Between sneezing fits I used the screwdriver to poke through the pile of dust and dog hair. No money.

Just then I heard a noise outside. I stood, clutching the screwdriver as if it were a knife. Silence. Had I imagined the noise?

What happened next was so fast that I couldn't believe it was happening. The unmistakable sound of the wooden bar sliding through the metal brackets told me that someone had locked me inside the shed. I opened my mouth to yell, but fortunately stopped myself. The door hadn't been barred accidentally. Whoever was out there had to have seen my car in the driveway. They also must have heard me sneeze repeatedly.

I picked up a shovel and very quietly took up a defensive position next to the door just in case the person decided to come back. I held my breath until I heard a car start. Then I gulped in air and stood there until the sounds of the engine faded.

With the immediate danger gone, I dropped the shovel and leaned against the wall as my knees threatened to buckle. Taking some deep breaths, I assessed my situation. My cell phone was in the car. I was dressed warmly, but the high at noon had been twenty-five degrees. By nightfall it would be several degrees colder, maybe even dip down into the single digits. *How long did it take for a person to freeze to death,* I wondered again. How long before the batteries in my flashlight died and I was in the dark? I shivered, more from fear than the cold.

Pull yourself together. This is a wooden shed, not a medieval fortress.

I forced myself to dismiss the possibility of death by cold and looked around. The old shed was constructed from wooden boards. Surely some had to be loose or damaged by the weather or even termites. But I had to work fast before I became too chilled.

After a few attempts of kicking against the boards with my feet, I discovered that this wasn't going to accomplish anything except exhaust me. The snow piled against the outside walls of the shed was too heavy. I would have to concentrate on the boards knee-high and up.

On the south wall the boards looked sturdy, but on the north side I saw water stains, suggesting that the roof leaked. The rain could have weakened the boards.

In the box of tools I found a sledgehammer. It was discouragingly heavy, but I managed to swing it against the weak board I had chosen. After three good whacks, the wood splintered. By the time I'd made a hole big enough to squeeze through, I was sweating. Crawling through the opening, I landed in the snow. The cold felt good, but I knew it was foolish to linger. Peering cautiously around the shed's corner, I saw no vehicle except my own. The person who'd imprisoned me was gone.

I examined the two sets of tracks around the door. My boots left a distinctive pattern. The other footprints were considerably larger, suggesting that they belonged to a man. Having established that, I ran to my car and took off for the agency.

Uncle Barney was back. I marched right past Lynn with a look that dared her to try to stop me. She didn't.

"Uncle Barney, do you have a minute?"

"Sure thing, Cybil." Then he looked up from the report he'd been reading and asked, "Are you all right? What happened?"

I collapsed into a chair and told him.

"I don't want you to drive to the Dwyer house alone again. And that's not open to negotiation."

"But that seriously affects my ability to do my job," I protested. "Besides, I don't think the man meant to kill me. If he had, he'd have used a much more direct method. He must have realized that I'd either get out of the shed or somebody would see my car and investigate."

"Why do you think he locked you up?"

"I've thought about that all the way back to town. I'm pretty sure I haven't annoyed anyone seriously enough to imprison me. So it must have been someone who had to look for something in the Dwyer house and didn't want to be seen or disturbed by me."

Barney nodded. "And you're sure it was a man?"

"From the size of his boot print I'd say it was a man."

Uncle Barney buzzed Glenn, who joined us immediately. I had to tell the story again. When I finished, Uncle Barney gave his orders.

"Glenn, you'll accompany Cybil if she needs to go out to the Dwyer place again. She's not to go there alone."

"Sure thing," Glenn said.

I shot him a dirty look for agreeing so readily. "I don't need a baby-sitter," I groused.

"How about an assistant?" Glenn said. "I talked to Louie the Lug. We're meeting him today."

"We?"

Glenn nodded. "I told you he was paranoid. Since he doesn't know you, I'll have to come along or it's no deal."

"Okay, you two settle this," Barney said.

Thus dismissed, we left the office.

"What are you cooking tonight?" Glenn asked me.

"I have a couple of nice chops—"

"With mashed potatoes? The kind you make from scratch?"

He was practically salivating. Since he and his wife had split up, I suspected that he lived on take-out and junk food. "Be at my house right after five. I'll teach you how to whip up mashed potatoes. It hardly takes a genius to make them."

"You mean that? About teaching me?"

"Yes. When do your cooking classes start?"

"In two weeks."

"Did you actually sign up?"

"Boy, you're suspicious." He whipped out his wallet and showed me the fee receipt.

"Now all you have to do is show up for classes and pay attention. Cooking isn't hard."

"That's the one thing I miss about my ex-wife."

"Her cooking?"

"Yes."

"See you after five at my house," I said and walked to my office.

Five minutes later my phone rang. "Louie the Lug will see us, but it has to be right now. Can you leave?" Glenn asked.

"Yes. I'll be right down."

We told Lynn we were on a case and left. "Shall we take my car or yours?" I asked.

"Neither. We walk."

"Louie the Lug lives near here?"

"I'm not sure where he sleeps. I doubt many people know. I told you he was paranoid. But he operates out of the back of the shoe repair shop."

I glanced at Glenn to be sure he was serious. He was. "If this were a movie or a crime novel, he'd operate out of the back of a seedy bar."

"Louie has a thing about shoes."

"A thing about shoes?"

"You'll see."

I wasn't so sure I wanted to see.

Chapter Eight

Louie the Lug sat on a slightly elevated platform that brought the shoeshine stand in front of him to chest level so he didn't have to bend down. He wore what I called farmer's overalls which were stretched to the ripping point across his melon-round belly. His thin gray hair was pulled back into a ponytail.

Glenn touched my arm. "We wait till he's finished with his customer."

We stood at a discreet distance. "Is it okay to watch?" I whispered.

"Sure."

Louie's cloth moved over the shoes at an awesome speed. In no time the customer's black wingtips looked as if they'd never been worn. The man dropped some bills into the three-pound coffee can next to Louie's chair and left. Louie's hands might have been too arthritic for fine forgeries, but he could still work magic on shoes. He fixed his pale-eyed gaze on us.

Glenn stepped forward and, after a few words, motioned me to join him. I handed the birth certificates to Louie, who studied them. The acrid smell of shoe polish hovered around him like an invisible shield.

What seemed mere seconds later, he handed them back. "As phony as a three-dollar bill. Whoever passed these off as acceptable should be flogged." His voice dripped with derision.

"They were made about seventeen years ago in this county. Any idea who was in the business back then?" Glenn asked.

"Seventeen years? That's quite a while."

Louie picked up a black penny loafer from the box beside him. His fingers moved lightly, caressingly over the leather while he was thinking. Finally he said, "A couple of names spring to mind. Frankie Flores and Billy Snider, but the longer I look at this document, the more it looks like Snider's work."

"Either of these gentlemen still around?" Glenn asked.

"Haven't seen Frankie in years. Last I heard, Billy lived over on Monroe Street in what used to be Mrs. Carruther's boarding house. Don't know what it's called now."

Glenn nodded. "I know the place." He dropped a twenty-dollar bill into the coffee can.

"Young lady," Louie said, addressing me for the first time, "those are nice boots but they need a shine badly."

He motioned for me to sit on a stool. I was about to refuse politely when Glenn's elbow poked my rib cage.
Obediently I sat down. "Shall I take them off?"

"Yes," Louie said.

Mentally I prepared myself for a longish session, but
Louie worked fast. I dug into my purse for my wallet
when Louie said Glenn had already paid. I had to admit
that the boots looked great and told him so. Louie smiled
broadly.

The men shook hands before we left.

"How come he didn't want to do your shoes?" I asked
Glenn.

"I come here regularly for a shine. Shall we walk over
to the old boarding house? It's now called a bed and
breakfast."

"That lovely Queen Anne mansion?"

Glenn shrugged. "Could be. I'm not familiar with ar-
chitectural styles."

The woman running the bed and breakfast informed us
frostily that since her house had been restored, they didn't
have any permanent residents. Theirs was not a rooming
house. If that's what we wanted, we could find one two
blocks south, on the other side of the tracks. The way the
corners of her mouth turned down clearly implied what she
thought of the other side of the tracks.

As soon as we crossed the railroad tracks which divided
the city in half, we found ourselves in a neighborhood pop-
ulated by the most recent immigrants and dominated by

abandoned buildings and rundown houses, bodegas, and Vietnamese grocery stores. Mercy Shelter was only a few blocks east. We were in familiar territory.

"The one ahead on the left is the only one big enough to be a rooming house," I said. "Let's try there."

The doorbell was broken so Glenn knocked forcefully.

"Hold your horses. I'm coming."

Moments later a big man jerked the door open and scowled at us.

"We didn't mean to be impatient," I said and offered a smile. He didn't smile back.

"What do you want?"

"A few words with Billy Snider."

"You cops?"

"No. We want to consult him about some documents."

"He's in the kitchen, fixing supper. Follow me."

We did and found Billy dunking slices of Spam into crushed saltine crackers before dropping them into a cast iron skillet. The grease hissed as the meat hit it.

"Mr. Snider, could you take a look at a couple of documents and tell us if you've seen them before? We're not cops. This is strictly a private matter," I said. Billy didn't even take his eyes off of the skillet for a second.

"Naturally we'll pay a consulting fee," Glenn added. That got Billy's attention.

He wiped his hands on a threadbare dishcloth before accepting the birth certificates. After squinting at them, he pulled a pair of wire-rimmed glasses from his shirt pocket. Then he nodded.

"Yeah, I remember these. Not my best work, but the woman was in a hurry." He handed them back.

"The woman? You remember her name? It's worth an extra bill," Glenn said.

"Her name was Shirley something. I remember because she wanted two sets of birth certificates."

"Two? Isn't that unusual?"

Billy shrugged as he flipped the slices of meat. "She was willing to pay for two sets, so I didn't care or ask questions."

"Did she tell you exactly what she wanted on them?"

"Yeah. Had it all written out for one and said to leave the other one blank except for the official's signature. Weird. But in my line of work I get lots of weird requests."

I just bet he did.

Money exchanged hands, and we left.

Walking back to the agency, we discussed what we'd learned. "Shirley Dwyer ordered two sets of birth certificates. Why two?"

Glenn shrugged. "To keep one set as insurance? Protection?"

"Liza told me that she had a twin sister who died hours after she was born. Stands to reason that Rose MacNiall was aware of the possibility that her daughter might be carrying twins. She must have told Shirley to get two certificates just in case."

"The MacNialls seem to be the kind of people who don't leave anything to chance," Glenn said with reluctant admiration.

"That still leaves us with the mystery of what happened to the other baby." We walked in silence for a while. Then I remembered something. "In the old days, people living on farms had their own small cemeteries. I wonder if that's still allowed and, if not, what the penalty is for burying a body in unconsecrated ground."

"I doubt that it's still allowed. It probably violates some health codes, so a fine is possibly the only consequence. We could look that up if it's important."

By the time we got back to the agency, we had just enough time to finish some paperwork before our cooking session. Except we never got around to that lesson.

Uncle Barney called us to his office. "I just found out that there's a house fire on London Street. The Washington sisters' place."

"We're on our way," Glenn said, hurrying out of the office.

I was right behind him. Driving to London Street, I tried to envision the house. Did the sisters have a fireplace? I didn't remember one in the living room, but they might have had a space heater or a wood burning stove, both of which caused many fires in our long winters.

The area was cordoned off to traffic, so we walked the last two blocks. We were almost at the house when I saw an ambulance speed away.

"I'll follow the ambulance to the hospital," I told Glenn.

"I'll stick around here. I know some of the firefighters."

On the way to the hospital, I dialed Luke's home

number. The machine kicked on, which meant he might be on duty.

I knew better than to barge into the emergency area and demand to see him. He would be busy. I forced myself to sit in the waiting room, turning the pages of an old copy of *Time* magazine. As per instructions posted on all walls, I'd turned my cell phone off. Yet I had to call Maxi and tell her about the fire. I dashed outside, not bothering to put on my coat. After the unusually cold spell we'd been having, it had finally warmed up a little. I raised my face to the sun in pure bliss.

Maxi was glad I'd phoned and said she'd leave for the hospital immediately. While I was outside, I called Glenn.

"I haven't been able to talk to the guys yet," he said. "They're still busy with the fire. All I know is that they put two women into the ambulance. I'll call as soon as I know anything more."

I told him I'd do the same thing.

Maxi arrived, carrying a picnic basket.

"You must have been speeding all the way," I said reprovingly.

"Only five miles over the limit. Sam told me officers didn't usually stop people who drove only a few miles faster than they were supposed to."

"Your cop grandson is a bad influence on you."

Maxi shrugged and grinned.

Luke walked into the waiting room. "Cybil, a nurse told me that you were here, but she didn't mention Maxi."

"I just got here."

Luke looked at us, obviously waiting for an explanation.

"The two women they brought in from the fire. How are they?" I asked.

"How do you know about them?"

Those eyes of his that rarely missed anything were focused on me. There were times when I liked being the center of Luke's attention, but this wasn't one of them. "They're part of the case I'm working on."

"That figures, though I was hoping you knew them from your charity work. Meals on Wheels or something like that."

"I know the Washington sisters too," Maxi said. "Will they be okay?"

"Probably, but we're keeping them for a day or two for observation. It's lucky that one of them woke up before they inhaled too much smoke."

"They were asleep?" I asked. "Wasn't it a little late in the afternoon for a nap?"

Luke shrugged. "Maybe they were tired and overslept."

"Most older people nap right after lunch so they don't spoil a good night's sleep," Maxi said thoughtfully.

She and I looked at each other. "You suppose someone gave them something to make them sleep through the fire?" I wondered out loud.

"That someone they had to talk to?"

"We'll know more as soon as we find out if this was a deliberately set fire or not," I said.

"Cybil, what are you involved in?" Luke demanded, scowling at me.

That hit me wrong. "Why don't you ask what those two sisters were involved in instead of questioning me?"

"Hey, hold on. I worry about you."

"You don't have to."

"I can't help myself, so sue me," he snapped.

Once again we'd reached this impasse where his need to be protective and my need to be independent collided.

"I brought food for an early supper," Maxi said. "Shall we go to the staff lounge to enjoy it?"

My grandmother the peacemaker.

"That sounds like a wonderful idea," Luke said, stepping between us. He placed one arm around Maxi's shoulders and one around mine.

When our eyes met, he flashed me a big smile. Though I loved his smile and found it disarming, I managed to give him a halfhearted I'll-get-you-for-this look.

The cafeteria was empty, which suited me. I was in no mood for small talk with any of Luke's colleagues I might encounter.

"What can I get you ladies to drink?" he asked.

"Their coffee is dreadful," Maxi said with a shudder.

"And the water is never hot enough to make a decent cup of tea," I added.

"That leaves milk or a soft drink," Luke said.

We each opted for a carton of skim milk.

From her basket Maxi removed linen napkins, utensils, and three wide-mouthed thermos bottles filled with a delicious vegetable stew. She served that with corn-and-cheese muffins. For Luke she'd brought a baggy filled with six almond-topped shortbread cookies.

"Maxi, you do everything with great style," Luke said.

"Thank you."

While we ate, my cell phone rang. I listened to Glenn's short report and suddenly was no longer hungry.

"What's wrong?" Maxi asked.

"The fire chief told Glenn that the fire had two points of origin."

"Oh, my," Maxi said.

Luke looked puzzled, so I explained. "It means that the fire started in two different places almost simultaneously and so spread very quickly."

He frowned. "How can it start in two places at almost the same time?"

"It can't unless someone set it deliberately."

"Someone tried to kill those two old ladies?" Luke asked, his voice disbelieving.

"Yes. We have to talk to them as soon as possible," I said.

Luke shook his head. "Not before tomorrow's visiting hours."

"I have to consult Uncle Barney." I left Maxi and Luke to finish their meal and hurried to the agency.

Uncle Barney was on the phone. While I waited, I organized my thoughts. When he was free, I told him succinctly what had happened.

"Two points of origin," he said thoughtfully. "A deliberately set fire, but by whom?"

I lifted my shoulders in a shrug. "Luke said the sisters won't be able to have visitors until tomorrow. I think I better join Glenn and see what's happening." Uncle Barney didn't discourage me.

When I got to the house on London Street, the firefighters were just finishing. Glenn was talking to the fire chief. I waited until they'd finished their conversation.

"The chief strongly suspects arson. Their investigator will run some tests for an accelerant as soon as the site has cooled down. He'll let me know what he finds."

"Accelerant?"

"Something to help spread the fire like gasoline or kerosene."

"Wouldn't the sisters have smelled something right away?"

"Not necessarily," Glenn said. "There are ways to delay the spread of a fire so that the person who set it isn't the obvious suspect. We'll know more after the arson investigator runs his tests."

I looked around. "Seems like most of the neighbors are standing outside, watching. Good time to ask some questions."

"Yeah. Like if anyone saw a stranger go into the house or lurking around."

"Would he or she take a chance on being seen?"

"Might not have had a choice." Glenn paused, thinking.

"What kind of people can go through a neighborhood without arousing suspicion?"

"Men or women who deliver things. Or read meters or repair things."

Glenn nodded.

"So, posing as one of these, our firebug could have gained entrance. In broad daylight Letty would have opened the door without suspicion to someone wearing a uniform or an official-looking work outfit. I know I would have."

"Me too. You want to take that side of the block, and I'll take this side?"

"Sure."

The first three people I talked with had been at work and had only returned in time to see the firefighters. The neighbor across the street had been at home and spoke with me on the porch. She hadn't heard anything until her son, who'd been playing outside, yelled for her to come and see the fire truck driving down their street.

"Did you see anyone going inside their house earlier?"

"No, but I was in the kitchen which faces the back."

I noticed that the boy was fidgeting the way kids do when they have something to say but are afraid to interrupt. I addressed his mother. "If you've seen anything at all, even if it seems trivial, it could help with our investigation." I hunkered down before I spoke to the boy directly. "Did you maybe look out the front window earlier?"

He nodded.

"Jimmy stayed home from school today. He wasn't feeling well this morning."

On cue, Jimmy produced a suspiciously fake cough.

"What did you see?"

"The man went into their house. The mean sister let him in."

"Jimmy, that's not a nice thing to say about Miss Letty."

"Mom, she *is* mean. She yells at us if our ball falls on her lawn, and at Halloween she gave me only one stick of gum."

"What did the man look like?" I asked.

"He was old."

"What was he wearing?"

"He looked like the guy who delivers packages," Jimmy said.

"The mailman?"

"No. I know the mailman."

He gave me the look kids reserve for particularly dense adults. It might have been the UPS or FedEx delivery man. "Did he have a package?"

Jimmy shook his head. "He had a big, black bag. Like the man who fixed our heater."

"And he went inside the house?"

Jimmy nodded.

"Did you see his van?"

"No. He didn't have one."

"When did he leave?"

The boy shrugged. "I dunno. I went to the kitchen to get a cookie."

"Thank you, Jimmy. You've been a great help."

The boy grinned proudly.

Glenn and I met at our cars. We sat in mine and compared notes. He hadn't learned a lot more than I had.

"A repairman without a truck," Glenn said and shook his head. "Those guys always park in front of the house or in the driveway. Yet nobody saw a truck."

"Jimmy said the man was old, but then he's probably only seven or eight and to a kid that age anyone over forty looks old."

"Except the next door neighbor also saw an elderly repairman go into the sisters' house. She was going out to get groceries and was planning to phone Letty later to ask if everything was okay."

"That's one brazen firebug. Or desperate. I wonder how he managed to set the fire with Letty in the house. Jane Ann isn't very mobile, but her sister is," I said.

"We'll find out tomorrow when we talk to the sisters. There isn't much more we can do here today."

"I'm going to pick up some food on the way home," I said. "We'll do the cooking lesson some other time if that's okay with you."

It was. We said good-bye and went our separate ways.

The next day I arrived at the hospital fifteen minutes before visiting hours began. I'd stopped at the florist's and picked up a pot of pink azaleas, which I placed on the night stand between the sisters' beds. They both thanked me profusely.

"How are you?" I asked, looking from one to the other.

"We've been better," Jane Ann said, her voice raspy.

"What happened?" I asked.

"There was a fire," Letty whispered.

Her nervous energy seemed to be depleted. "Did your smoke alarm go off?"

"Only the one by the attic door," Jane Ann said. "And that's weird because Letty replaced the batteries in both of them last week. The alarm by the basement door should have gone off as well."

"My colleague knows the fire chief. I'll have him mention this. Your neighbor said that you had a visitor earlier that day. A repairman?"

"He wasn't a repairman," Letty said. "He was from the gas company. He came to check the furnace downstairs."

"Did you go down with him?"

"No," Letty said. "I sprained my ankle a couple of days ago and couldn't climb the stairs."

"Have either of you seen this man before?" Both shook their heads.

"Can you describe him?"

"I'd say he was close to retirement age. Tall. Distinguished-looking," Jane Ann said.

"And he had a mustache. The droopy kind. Sort of like a walrus," Letty added.

"Did he have an accent?"

"Yes, but it was weird," Letty said. "I couldn't make up my mind whether it was a Spanish or a German accent."

"Did he go anywhere else in the house?" I asked.

"Yes, the kitchen. He wanted to check our cooking stove. It's gas," Letty said.

"Did you go with him?"

"No, my foot—"

"Did you hear him open the refrigerator?"

"Well, yes." Letty clapped her hand over her mouth in the age-old gesture of shocked surprise. "He asked if he could get a drink of water. I said yes and that we kept a pitcher of filtered water in the ice box."

"Did you both drink water from the pitcher after he left?"

"Yes. You think he put something into the water?" Jane Ann asked.

"I don't know, but it would explain why you almost slept through the smoke alarm going off." I paused before asking the question I'd come to ask. "I know the forty-eight hours aren't quite up yet, but did you have a chance to talk to that certain person about the adoption seventeen years ago?"

They were prevented from answering by another visitor who turned out to be the arson investigator. I wished them a speedy recovery and told them I'd be back the next day.

In the meantime, Glenn had returned to the agency.

"That fire was definitely arson," he said. "They found

candlewax in the basement. Candlewax hardly ever burns up completely in a fire."

He looked at me as if this was self-explanatory. When I made a please-continue gesture, he explained.

"You set a candle inside a cardboard box and place it near something flammable. Like drapes or a stack of newspapers or cleaning supplies. You put paper strips around the candle and douse the paper with an accelerant. You light the candle. When it burns down, it'll ignite the paper and in no time you've got a good flame going."

"It's that simple?"

Glenn nodded. "The size of the candle lets you choose how soon the fire starts. A votive candle for quick fires and a big fat one for a long delay."

"Allowing the firebug to establish an alibi. Clever."

"Now all we need is a motive," Glenn said.

"The fire starter didn't want the sisters to talk to someone about a certain adoption."

"The question is why?"

I shrugged. "I'll go back to speak to the sisters again."

"Make it soon."

"I know. Whoever meant for them to die in the fire may try again."

"Not may. Will," Glenn claimed.

"I'll go back during the evening visiting hours."

Promptly at seven I entered the sisters' hospital room to be confronted by two stripped beds. "What on earth?"

I murmured, anxiety shooting through me. I ran to the nurses' station.

"The Washington sisters. Their beds are stripped. What happened to them?"

"Take it easy. It's not what you think. They left," the nurse on duty said.

"What do you mean, they left?"

"They got dressed and walked out of here. Didn't wait for the doctor to discharge them. Didn't even tell me they were leaving."

"That's bad. Really bad," I said and had to lean against the wall.

"Yes, it is. They were supposed to stay another day or two. They didn't get their dinner or their evening meds. Or the pills they were supposed to take with them when they went home."

"Did they leave by themselves? Did someone come to pick them up?"

"I don't know. I didn't see them leave. We were getting ready to deliver dinner trays."

"Who else was on the floor then?"

"The nurse helping me and a couple of nursing students."

"Are they still here?"

"The students are. They're probably in the staff lounge studying."

"Could I talk to them?"

"Just knock on the staff room door."

"Thank you."

Chapter Nine

The girls, two sleep-deprived looking nineteen-year olds, agreed to speak with me, though they said they really had to study for an organic chemistry test. I promised to be brief.

"You have my sympathy. Chemistry was not my favorite subject."

"Tell us about it," Ashley, the ponytailed brunet, said with an impressive eyeroll.

We chatted for a moment longer before I asked the questions I'd come to ask. "Can you describe the man who came to pick up the Washington sisters? Did they seem glad to see him?"

"Not really. I had the feeling they might have been a little afraid of him," the other student said. "You know, like someone you're intimidated by."

"What did he look like?"

"Old, but he moved with energy," Ashley said. "And he had a droopy mustache."

"Droopy? Like a walrus?" I asked.

She giggled. "Yeah, exactly."

"What about his hair?"

"He wore a cap. Like a baseball cap. What I could see of his hair, it was mostly white, long, and stringy."

"What was he wearing?"

"An old overcoat. Dark gray."

"Were his clothes shabby? Well-worn? New?"

"Shabby. Except his shoes."

I waited for an explanation.

"Joni's family owns a shoe store, so she knows shoes," Ashley said.

"They weren't new, but they were expensive. Italian. They, like, made me think that at some time in his life he must have been well-off. Know what I mean?"

When I nodded, she continued.

"Those kinds of shoes are expensive but last a long time."

The shoes must have been his own as it was lots easier to find clothes than shoes that fit in a secondhand store. The clothes along with the walrus mustache convinced me that they were part of a disguise. But why the need for a disguise? Unless he was a public figure or someone whose photo appeared in the newspapers or on television from time to time?

I thanked the girls and left them bent over their chemistry notes.

I drove straight to the Washington house on the off-chance that the sisters had been taken there. When I saw the house, I realized that the fire and water damage was extensive enough to call for major repairs or perhaps even complete demolition.

Not knowing where to look for them, I drove to the agency where we met for a short conference. Lynn served mugs of coffee.

"According to the fire chief, there were no batteries in the fire alarm on the main floor," Glenn said.

"That's impossible. Letty replaced them recently," I said.

"The fake repair man could have removed them," Uncle Barney speculated, "before he set the fire."

"But why?" Glenn wondered out loud.

"Obviously the sisters know something somebody doesn't want us to find out," I said. "And that person spirited them out of the hospital, possibly against their will."

"We have no proof of that," Glenn said.

"No, but they weren't scheduled to be released for another day or two. I seriously doubt that they were in any shape to take care of themselves. Remember, I saw them."

"But to practically abduct them from the hospital—"

"Glenn, how hard could it be to intimidate two elderly ladies into leaving the hospital who'd just been through the trauma of a fire?" I asked.

"You're right," he agreed. "But where could he have taken them?"

"A place that's difficult to get into," Uncle Barney said.

"Like the MacNiall place. A tall stone wall. A security gate. Surveillance cameras. And two aggressive dogs," I said.

"Still, the place is not impossible to get into," Glenn maintained.

"If we could get past the gate and the dogs—"

"How did you get past them last time?" Glenn asked.

"We had an appointment with Rose MacNiall." Then the solution hit me. "We have to deliver our biweekly report. That'll get us through the gate. There's a longish, curving drive up to the house—"

"The car slows down, and I jump out from under the blanket on the floor—"

"Not just you. Me too," I said. "That garden is big. It'll take time to search it." We both stopped and looked at Uncle Barney.

He seemed to be deep in thought. I wondered if he'd heard me. He tapped the stem of his unlit pipe against his teeth. "That still leaves the problem of the dogs."

Glenn spoke up. "We could toss slabs of meat at them which would keep them occupied. We could rub crushed sleeping pills on the meat for an instant siesta."

"I remember seeing one of those nature programs where the vet shot the mountain lion or the cougar or whatever the big cat was called with a tranquilizer gun so he could examine it. I bet our zoo has one of those. Uncle Barney, aren't you on the board of directors of the zoo?"

He nodded. "But I'm not going to ask the director for the loan of one of those guns. First, I doubt he'd lend me one and second, it would be taking unethical advantage of my position on the board."

The intercom buzzed. "I have to take this call," Uncle Barney said.

Glenn and I left his office.

After a few minutes he called us back. "That was Rose MacNiall. She's coming for an update on the case."

"There goes our plan for getting into the mansion," I said.

"Do we need to sit in?" Glenn asked.

"No, thank you."

"Want to get some coffee?" Glenn asked, "and consider alternate plans?"

"Come to my office. I'll make some. It's better than the stuff Lynn made this morning." I had one of those little machines that brewed one cup at a time. I gave the first one to Glenn.

Leaning back in my chair, I asked, "Well?" I blew on my coffee to cool it.

"What?"

"Among your . . . um . . . colorful acquaintances who all seem to have access to guns, there isn't one who could lay his hands on a tranquilizer gun?"

"Probably, but it wouldn't be cheap. And I don't know if Barney would approve."

That was true. The agency's policy was to stick as close to the law as possible unless one of us was in mortal danger. Or if there was absolutely no other way, and then we could only "bend" the law a little in our quest to help someone. "The only other thing I can think of is that one of us keeps the dogs busy by the front gate while the other climbs over the wall and searches."

"What all is in that garden?"

"There's a hothouse and a shed that I know of. The rest is trees and flowers and shrubs and lawn. Maybe an herb garden. And there's a swimming pool and tennis courts."

"A lot to search."

"Not that much. We can rule out everything except the hothouse. It's the only one that would be heated."

"You've been to the house. Did you see the backyard? What's the layout?"

I closed my eyes and pictured what I'd seen when we waited to be admitted to the house. "The pool is right behind the patio, and the tennis court is farther back and to the left. The shed and the hothouse are in the very back, near the wall."

"So, if they were hidden or hiding out on the estate, they'd probably be in the hothouse or the main house," Glenn said.

"The house is huge. I'm sure it has a basement and the kind of attic in which you can stand up. Lots of places to hide someone."

"Or keep them against their will," Glenn said.

"Maybe we're making this too complicated. Since

their house was badly damaged, maybe they checked into a motel or are staying with friends or relatives. Their reasons for leaving the hospital don't have to be sinister."

"True."

"But?"

"There's that fake gas company employee who disarmed the smoke alarm and set the fire which was meant to kill them."

"There's that," I agreed with a sigh. "The only reason he didn't succeed is because he was an amateur, thank heaven."

"Definitely an amateur," Glenn agreed. Summing up, he said, "We have a guy who's tall and in his mid-sixties."

"And he's distinguished-looking and carries himself well."

"Have we come across anyone like that in this case?"

We both thought for a moment. "Merritt Barton is too young for the part."

"And why would he need the masquerade?" Glenn asked.

"Dr. Ralph Gideon is too old and physically wrong for the part. Francis MacNiall is the right age, but why would he put on a disguise or be mixed up with the Washington sisters? Let's face it, Glenn. As far as the motive for eliminating Letty and Jane Ann is concerned, we have no clue. But we have to find them."

Glenn nodded. "I'll see what I can do about a tranquilizer gun."

"Okay, but before we do anything drastic, let me ask

Maxi to check around. She goes to the same church as the sisters. They could be staying with friends."

Glenn left to meet his shady cronies, and I phoned my grandmother who promised to call her church friends.

An hour later she called back.

"No one has seen Letty and Jane Ann, and they didn't come to the Wednesday evening service, which is most unusual. They rarely miss it and, when they do, they phone to say that the church bus shouldn't come to pick them up. This time they didn't phone and weren't there when the bus came. Cybil, I'm worried."

"Me too."

"What are you going to do?" Maxi asked.

"First, call all the motels and hotels to be sure they didn't check into one of them."

"That's quite a job. I'll help. How are we going to do it?"

I considered her offer for a moment. Since I couldn't see any danger in her making some phone calls, I could use her help. "I could pretend to be a florist with a delivery whose less-than-competent helper hadn't gotten the right motel for the sisters. You could say that two members of your church lost their home in a fire and you're trying to locate them to bring them some cookies or a cake."

"Cookies," Maxi said. "I have some in the freezer which I could actually deliver to the sisters when we find them."

"Sounds good. You have your phone book handy?"

"Yes."

I told her the page number of the motel listings. "You want to take A through K, and I'll take the rest?"

"Fine," she said eagerly.

"Oma, this is going to take time," I warned.

"I had nothing planned for today. Let's do it."

Maxi called me just after I'd finished my part of the phone interviews. Neither one of us had located the sisters.

"Now what?" Maxi asked.

"Who are the people who'd be most interested in the Washington sisters' disappearance?"

Maxi thought for a minute. "The people who adopted Chelsea or someone in the MacNiall family."

"Yes. Since we don't know who adopted the baby—"

"We'll concentrate on the MacNialls. Rose doesn't know or she wouldn't have hired you to find her granddaughter."

"By all accounts her mother-in-law was the control freak of the family. I can't believe she didn't know who adopted her great granddaughter."

"And she would have kept a record or told someone in the family. She wouldn't have confided in Rose, who was an outsider, but she would have told a true MacNiall," Maxi said.

"That's what I'm thinking too."

"So, the sisters might be hiding out on the MacNiall estate."

"Yes. We have to search the hothouse. From what Liza told me, it has a small living area at one end. The gardener isn't there at this time of the year."

"The problem is how to get in," Maxi mused.

"Yes. Glenn and I have to find a way to get over the wall." I told Maxi about the dogs.

"Count me in. Now don't say no. Do you know anyone who can appear more confused and dithery than I?" she asked with a hint of pride. "You need a lookout and someone to distract the dogs. I'm perfect for the part. I'll be this little old lady who pulls up to the gate because she's lost her way and needs directions to Applegate Road, which is nearby." She paused for a moment. "Are you thinking of tranquilizing the dogs?"

My mouth dropped open in surprise. Sometimes we were so on the same page it was scary. "Glenn is out there now, trying to get the right stuff."

"Be sure you give them the correct dosage. You don't want them to wake up too soon."

The idea of being chased by those two large, snarling dogs made a shiver run down my spine.

"When were you thinking of executing this plan?" she asked.

"Executing? That sounds like a military operation. And with what's at stake, we should probably treat it as such."

"When?"

"Tomorrow. Either just before first light or at dusk. We need some light so we don't have to use flashlights which could be spotted, but shadowy enough so that if someone looks out into the backyard, we don't stand out like beacons."

"Call me as soon as you know zero hour."

Later that evening Glenn phoned. He'd scored the tranquilizer gun and the drugs. He assured me he had the correct dosage. We planned our strategy before I called Maxi.

"We're on for tomorrow evening at five. We'll meet on Crocus Lane, just east of the old fire station."

"Roger. Seventeen hundred hours at check point Crocus."

I chuckled. Nobody could get into a role the way Maxi could. "Oma, don't overdo the dithery little old lady act."

"Are you accusing me of overacting? Shame on you, Cybil. Have I ever done that?"

In response to my laughter, she said, "Don't answer that. I'll be convincing and believable."

"Please remember that two people have been murdered and two have disappeared. We're dealing with a dangerous person. Or persons."

Subdued, she said, "I know. I pray that Letty and Jane Ann are alive and well."

Since Merritt Barton wanted a more thorough investigation of his son's girlfriend, I thought it best to meet her.

As I'd been a guidance counselor with the Westport school system, I was still on their volunteer/substitute list. I called them and indicated that I had some time and was interested in volunteering at the grade school nearest my house, which happened to be Samuel Adams Elementary School—Annette Ferris's place of employment. I added that I had a particular fondness for fifth-graders.

That evening I found a message on my machine from the school that if I had any time in the next three weeks, the fifth-grade teacher could use help as the students were starting a big project in social studies.

Next morning the principal took me to Annette Ferris's room and introduced me. I prayed that she wouldn't recognize me as the woman who had offered help the night Perry drove off the road. She didn't. I sat with her at her desk while the children finished their math worksheets.

On the desk next to a felt-covered coffee can filled with crayons and pencils sat a framed photograph. "Your family?"

"Yes. Mom and Dad and my sister, Ceecee."

I could see a resemblance between Annette and her mother but none to Ceecee. Yet the longer I looked at the young girl, the more familiar she seemed. I didn't think I'd met her, but she reminded me of someone. Annette's voice distracted me.

"They studied Indiana last year, so I'll eliminate it from the choices," she said in a low voice.

"Are you going to let them choose their state?"

"No. I did that last year and inevitably several kids

wanted the same state which led to endless squabbling. I could assign the states alphabetically—"

"Or let them pick a state from a hat. I've seen this method work quite well."

"Let's do that."

Annette printed the names of the states on slips of paper, which I folded and put into a small basket on her desk. She had just collected the math papers when she was summoned to the office.

"Mrs. Quindt, would you mind conducting the drawing?"

"Not at all." Using her seating chart, I called the students up to the desk. I entered the name of the state they drew next to their names. Inevitably there were some complaints.

"I don't want Illinois. The Cubs stink," a little red-haired imp declared.

"Trade you for Mississippi?"

"I'll give you Maine?"

"Children," Annette admonished as she reentered the classroom. "There will be no trades. I bet each one of you will discover something new and interesting about your state. We'll line up and go to the library after you print the name of your state on the folder I gave you yesterday."

After several minutes of searching for the folder and a pencil, we were ready to go.

"Is there anyone in particular you want me to help?"

Annette looked over her class and nodded. "See the boy in the last row next to the window?"

I nodded.

"That's Toby. He's always been a bit of a loner, but he's been even more withdrawn lately. I haven't figured out what's wrong. I've kept an eye on him. The kids haven't picked on him, so I suspect it's something at home."

I followed the kids to the media center where the librarian had placed several sets of encyclopedias and state books on a cart for us. Pulling out a chair near Toby's table, I waited until he'd selected the *M* volume of *World Book*. When I observed him doodling on his note paper and staring at the open encyclopedia, I moved my chair closer.

"Missouri? Interesting state," I said quietly.

He shrugged.

"Ever been there?"

He shook his head.

"In St. Louis they have this tall arch down by the Mississippi that you can go up in. Great view. Of course, when it's windy, the arch sways." I made a side-to-side motion with my hands. "That can be scary."

"I wouldn't be scared," he maintained stoutly.

"I believe you wouldn't be. Now let's find a picture of the arch."

The day seemed long and yet when the dismissal bell rang, I was surprised. I walked the kids to their bus. On the way back, Annette thanked me for helping her and invited me back any day I had some time.

"I think I know what might be bothering Toby. When we were looking through the stack of magazine pictures, he stopped to stare at a picture of a baby. Later I found that picture crumpled up on the floor. What do you know about his family?"

Annette stopped in her tracks. "At our parent-teacher conference I believe his mom mentioned that they were adopting a baby girl. That can be quite traumatic. I know I felt shaken and unsure of my parents' love when they adopted my sister. I was about the same age as Toby."

"You obviously adjusted."

"Yes, but it took a few weeks of sulking and resenting. Now I can't imagine life without Ceecee. She's a senior in high school."

"Are your parents teachers too?"

"No. Dad's a claims adjuster and Mom's a pharmacist."

Annette thanked me again before we parted.

Driving to the agency, something she'd said kept nagging at me, but I was too keyed up by our upcoming visit to the MacNiall place to capture the elusive associative thought.

Glenn was waiting for me at the agency.

"I checked with my contact in the police department. They have no leads on the sisters' whereabouts. They are now considered officially missing."

"They didn't just disappear into thin air," I muttered. Not knowing what else to do, I said, "Let's go over the plan again." Glenn had made coffee, which was actually drinkable. I thanked him for it.

"First, Maxi provides some kind of distraction at the front gate while I tranquilize the dogs."

"Hold on. The dogs have to come to the gate and raise the alarm when Maxi's there or the guard will become suspicious. You have to tranquilize them afterwards."

He nodded. "That's assuming that the guard goes back into his hut and the dogs locate us on top of the back wall. That's a little risky, isn't it?"

"Yes, but can you think of an easier way to get in?"

"If it were summer, I could claim to be the gardener's new assistant—"

"That gives me an idea on how we can gain entry into the mansion."

"How?"

"We're a cleaning team sent on a promotional service. We do a free cleaning and have an estimate of how much it would cost to clean the house. No obligation."

Glenn frowned. "Are you hinting we actually have to clean? I hate cleaning!"

"Nobody loves it, but we'd do only a couple of rooms," I promised. "Then in order to give an estimate, one of us has to look at the rooms while the other one sneaks off to look for traces of the Washington sisters."

"I'm not crazy about this plan," Glenn protested.

"Tell you what. You do the vacuuming. I'll do the dusting."

"Thanks a lot," he groused. Looking at his watch, he said, "It's time to rock and roll."

I ran into the bathroom and changed into a navy sweat suit, a dark green jacket, and work boots.

Glenn loaded the truck with a ladder.

When he saw my questioning look, he said, "How else can we get over the wall? It's been years since I was in the Army and had to scale a wall. And then I had a rope and a grappling hook."

"The ladder's a good idea," I conceded. "I've never scaled a wall. What's in the bag?"

"The tranquilizer gun and a couple of drug-infused pieces of beef as a backup."

I nodded my approval.

We waved at Maxi—who was parked near the mansion—and proceeded to drive out of sight. We left the truck and trudged through the snow with the ladder. I carried the meat.

Glenn let me climb up on the ladder for a quick look into the backyard. The first thing I saw were the upturned faces of the dogs. I almost fell off the ladder when they jumped halfway up the wall, barking like crazy. I ducked out of sight when I saw the door of the guard's hut open.

"Are you barking at them squirrels again, you mangy mutts?" he yelled. "Knock it off and get over here." He blew his whistle.

I waited several seconds before I risked another look. The dogs had retreated toward the hut, but when they saw me, they came running back. The guard yelled at them again to shut up. They did, but stayed just on the other side of the wall.

"We'll have to wait for Maxi's diversion." I glanced at my watch. "She should be at the front gate any second now."

I perched on the wall to give Glenn a chance to look at the terrain. The dogs sat like two deadly statues, looking at us with unblinking eyes.

A second before I heard the commotion at the front gate, the dogs did and took off toward the wrought-iron entrance.

"Maxi's arrived," I said.

"Hope she didn't slide into the gate and damage her truck."

"She's driven on snowy roads for the last fifty years. She can handle them."

We watched the guard give the quiet command to the dogs and speak to Maxi. We were too far away to hear the conversation. After Maxi left and the guard went back inside his hut, we decided to start Operation Hothouse.

Glenn positioned the ladder against the inside wall for a fast, or faster, getaway.

"Here come the dogs," he said, getting his tranquilizer gun ready. He hit the front dog but missed the one behind him. I got out the doctored slab of sirloin and tossed it as far away from the ladder as I could.

"Good throw," Glenn said.

The dog ran after it, and after sniffing it for a second, started to devour the meat in big gulps.

"I hope the tranquilized meat takes effect before the other dog wakes up," I said.

"Me too. I can't believe I missed that mutt."

"You had a relatively small moving target and poor light. I think you did well to have hit one of them," I said consolingly.

"Look, dog number two is getting drowsy."

We watched him lie down, waited another minute, and then climbed down the ladder.

Keeping to the edge of the property, we ran in a crouch to the hothouse. The door was unlocked, and we slipped inside. It was now dark enough that we needed our flashlights. We kept our beams pointed downward.

The hothouse contained a number of plants that had been moved inside for the winter. The place smelled of earth and spring. "I can't wait for spring," I murmured yearningly.

"Less than a month and the snow will be gone," Glenn said. "Maybe sooner."

We made our way to the far end. It contained a sofa, a table and chairs, a small fridge, and a hot plate on a small counter.

"All the comforts of home," Glenn muttered. He moved the couch cushions. "What's this?" he asked, holding up a long bobby pin.

I grabbed it and looked at it. "Letty uses pins like these to hold her hair back. I remember because they're always slipping out of that untidy bun on her head."

"Proves she was here," Glenn said. "The question is, where is she now?"

"After the MacNialls have left for the office tomorrow

morning, the Speedy Cleaning Service will arrive at the mansion for the complimentary cleaning they won in a raffle," I said.

Glenn groaned. "Don't tell me we're this cleaning service, and I'm part of the mop brigade."

"You are our master vacuumer."

"And what will you be doing?"

"Wearing my curly Orphan Annie wig and tinted glasses and doing the dusting."

"Do I need a disguise?" Glenn asked.

"No. You haven't been in the house before. And we're both going to be doing more snooping than cleaning. I wonder if Maxi might want to come along."

"Probably. Now we better get out of here before those dogs wake up."

"Right." In my excitement over finding the pin, I'd forgotten about the slumbering dogs.

Glancing at my watch, I asked, "How long are the tranquilizers effective?"

"I'm not sure since I had to guess the dogs' weights. I hope I erred on the side of safety."

"You're telling me now that those beasts could wake up any moment?"

"Let's go," he said and started to run. "Keep to the wall till we reach the ladder."

Good advice since it was now almost completely dark. Using the wall as a guide, I ran through the remnants of the heavy, wet snow, which sucked at my shoes like wet cement. As I kept looking for signs of the dogs, I didn't see the object in front of me until I ran into it. I grabbed it to steady myself and saw that what my hands had latched onto was a small statue of a stone angel. The MacNialls weren't known for being particularly religious, so why a statue of an angel? "Shades of Thomas Wolfe," I muttered. Hearing a commotion in front of me, and seeing a smaller shadow lunge after the larger one which I assumed to be Glenn, I cried out.

"Glenn? What's going on?"

"The first dog woke up. Get over the fence while I feed him the other piece of meat."

Increasing my speed until I thought my lungs would burst, I reached the ladder. My first attempt to get on it failed due to the snow crusted on my boots. Hearing Glenn behind me, I gained a foothold and clambered up. I fell rather than jumped over the wall. Moments later Glenn was up on the wall, throwing the ladder over to our side. The dog barked furiously. We heard the guard's whistle just as Glenn jumped down and landed beside me.

"Good thing the snow acts as a cushion," he wheezed. "The dogs were supposed to be out longer. I guess I underestimated their weight."

"Let's get out of here. I don't want another encounter with the Baskerville's hounds."

Neither did Glenn. We beat a hasty, undignified retreat.

Chapter Ten

Barely recovered from our clandestine visit to the Mac-Niall estate, Maxi, Glenn, and I met on Crocus Lane at first light. We took turns yawning prodigiously.

"Let me see what those shirts look like," Maxi said, who posed as the boss of our company, the Speedy Cleaning Service.

We unbuttoned our coats. "When did you have time to embroider the logo on the pockets of these denim shirts?" I asked.

"Did two last night after you phoned and one this morning. Hmm," she said, looking critically at us. "Glenn's shirt is a little snug and yours a little too big. Wear them unbuttoned over your T-shirts."

Maxi had tied a gray scarf around her white hair just in case the same guard was on duty who'd seen her before.

We sat in Glenn's truck until the two MacNiall cars passed on their way to the offices. Maxi looked at the IDs and Speedy Cleaning Service papers Glenn had run off on his computer. Armed with these, we drove to the mansion and told the guard that Mrs. MacNiall had hired us. He phoned the house and then admitted us. We heard the dogs bark but didn't see them, which was fine with me.

The same grumpy housekeeper let us in, professing that she knew nothing of a cleaning crew. Maxi convinced her that Rose had approved our visit for a service estimate. The housekeeper's dour expression brightened considerably.

"I've been trying to tell her to hire a service. There's too much work for me in a house this size, and the daily help from town is practically worthless." She harrumphed, underscoring her opinion of the town help. "Where do you want to start?"

"Let's begin with upstairs and work our way down," Maxi said.

We'd agreed that the sisters wouldn't be hidden in the family quarters. As the housekeeper and Maxi inspected the rooms on the left side of the long hall, I opened the narrow door on the far end. I motioned for Glenn to join me.

"Stairs to the attic," he murmured.

"Why don't you vacuum the nearest room and keep an eye on the housekeeper? If she heads this way, turn off the machine briefly and turn it on again. Do that twice to warn me."

"Okay. Good luck."

I slipped up the steep stairs to a finished attic. In bygone days of live-in servants, they probably slept up here. Quickly I searched the rooms. Under one of the beds I found an empty vial of insulin. I was fairly certain that it was the same brand I'd seen on Jane Ann's end table. Using a tissue, I picked it up. Before I could slip it into my pocket, a tall body stepped in front of me.

"What are you doing up here?" the man demanded.

Hot fear shot through me. I had to swallow before I could speak. Though I recognized him from his newspaper photos, I pretended not to. "Your wife . . . your wife asked us to look at the house to estimate how much a biweekly cleaning would cost," I said, opening my eyes wide to look as innocent as I could. I curled one hand around the vial while lifting the basket with my cleaning supplies up higher for him to see. The smell of ammonia wafted from it, causing him to step back. As he did, I pushed the vial into my pocket.

"She's my sister-in-law, not my wife, and I doubt she meant to include this floor in the biweekly cleaning."

"Mrs. MacNiall said top to bottom. Now you made me lose count of the number of rooms up here," I said, my voice filled with petulant complaint.

"There are six rooms and one bathroom. Now you can go back down."

Francis MacNiall stepped closer, forcing me toward the stairs. "But I have to see the rooms."

"Six rooms and a bath. That's all you need to know."

He forced me to take another step back. For a panic-filled moment I wondered if he would push me down the stairs if I didn't leave. The expressionless, cold face and the ferretlike eyes hinted that he was capable of just that. I turned and hastened down. At the bottom I turned and looked back. He was still standing there, motionless, watching me. I didn't exactly run to the front door but I didn't saunter either. Glenn followed me, lugging the vacuum cleaner. A few seconds later, Maxi joined us.

"Let's get out of here," I said and opened the door.

Following close behind me, Maxi asked, "What happened?"

"We were wrong in assuming that both MacNialls had left. Francis cornered me up there and ordered me to leave. If I hadn't, I think he might have pushed me down the stairs." I shivered.

"He must have been up there already," Glenn said. "He didn't go up after you did. I was at the bottom of those stairs the whole time."

"What was he doing up there?" Maxi asked, her voice thoughtful. "According to the housekeeper, the family doesn't use the third floor."

"What didn't he want me to see? What or who's up there?" I wondered out loud. "We blew our one chance to find out."

"That's not your fault, Cybil," Maxi said.

After we got into the truck, I said, "Let's park on Crocus Lane to regroup." After we parked, I pulled the vial from my pocket. "I'm pretty sure I saw the same vial on Jane Ann's table."

Maxi looked at it. "That's a very common brand of insulin. You can even get it through the mail."

"Still, it's a coincidence and you know how much I distrust coincidences."

"We've got to get back into that house," Maxi said.

"But this time we'll make sure Francis isn't at home." A little of the metallic taste of fear still lingered in my mouth. I so didn't want to meet him on top of a steep staircase again.

"The old guy really got to you," Glenn said.

"He isn't that old and there's something scary about him. An aura of cold, controlled menace." I could feel both of them looking at me.

"You're usually way too unafraid to suit me," Maxi said, "so if you're scared now, there's a good reason for it. I'll have to take a closer look at this Francis MacNiall."

"What do you want to bet that most of the time he's the picture of elegant urbanity and sophistication."

Neither of them took me up on a bet.

"So, what do we do now?" Glenn asked.

"Park on Locust Lane and wait and watch. When the coast is clear, we'll go back. Tell the housekeeper we forgot to check something," I said.

"This time I'll hide in the ditch across from the gate so that I can see who's in the cars leaving the estate," Glenn said. "When it's him, I'll signal you to come."

I shook my head. "Don't you think he'll have left instructions with the guard not to let us back in?"

"Probably. We'll have to think of something else," Glenn agreed gloomily.

"If I could speak to the housekeeper alone, I could get some information out of her," Maxi said.

She probably could. People, often complete strangers, confided in Maxi. As we sat there, I wondered what all a housekeeper did. "You suppose she does the grocery shopping for the household?"

"Probably. And she'd do it in the morning. Good thinking, Schatzi."

"So, we'll wait here and follow her. I saw a station wagon parked in the back. I bet that's what she drives."

Since none of us could think of a better plan, we agreed on this one. Glenn sprinted to the ditch from where he had a good view of the gate while Maxi and I waited in the truck.

Thirty minutes later he came running back. "She just left in the station wagon, heading east," he said breathlessly.

"What's east of here?" Maxi asked.

"The new shopping mall, which has, among other things, a grocery store, a deli, and a liquor store." Glenn started the truck and turned east.

By driving ten miles above the speed limit, we spotted the station wagon before it reached the shopping center. He parked in the row behind it.

"You two stay here," Maxi said. "I'll see what information I can pry out of her."

We sat in silence. I shivered.

"Are you cold? I could run the engine for a while."

"I'm not cold." That was a lie, but in long silences my thoughts often drifted to my sweet little boy. Losing him had put the kind of coldness into my heart that all the heaters in the world could not defeat.

To distract myself from my sadness, I picked up the morning paper. Glenn asked for the crossword puzzle. Handing it to him, I repressed a sigh. I knew that in a minute or so, he'd ask for help. It took only thirty seconds.

"What does *telic* mean?"

"Something that has a purpose."

"Hmm. Purposeful fits. Thanks." He filled in the spaces. "How do you know all those odd words?"

"From doing lots of crossword puzzles." After my darling son died, the only thing that could distract my tormented mind and soul were puzzles. Luke used to bring me puzzles by the dozen. Remembering also made me think of my estranged husband. I wondered if that cute young nurse had been back to his apartment.

"What's the matter?" Glenn asked.

"Nothing. Why?"

"You're beating your fists against the seat."

I looked down and saw that my hands were actually clenched into fists. This was not good. Had I, by suggesting that we live apart for a while, given him tacit permission to see other women? I had not meant to do that. Absolutely not. Luke was still my husband and thus off limits to some eyelash-batting, doctor-adoring, barely-out-of-training nurse. I might have to look her up and tell her that.

"Here comes Maxi. From the way she moves, she learned something," he said.

Maxi scooted in next to me. She looked at each of us and grinned.

"The cat that ate the canary has nothing on you. Spill it, Oma."

"The MacNialls have a summer cottage on Bear Lake."

"Bear Lake? Where's that?" I asked.

"It's one of the five small lakes near here," Glenn said. "It has cottages all around it."

It was near the lake I'd been dumped in on my last major case. The memory made me shiver. Pulling myself together, I glanced at my watch. "Liza should be at her desk by now. She should be able to give us directions and a description of the cottage."

Using my cell, I phoned her. She didn't ask for an explanation but gave me instructions, which I wrote on the back of a bank deposit slip.

"Thanks, Liza. I'll get back to you."

"Let's go," Maxi said. "I doubt that the cottage is heated well and old people don't tolerate the cold."

"Step on it, Glenn." I hoped we wouldn't be too late to rescue the sisters.

"Why do you suppose he took the sisters to that cottage?" Glenn wondered.

"Maybe someone in the house became suspicious, and he had no choice," I said.

"I'm surprised they're still alive," Glenn said.

I thought about that. "I suspect they haven't told him what he wants to know."

"The name of the couple who adopted Chelsea?" Maxi asked.

"Yes. Oma, you know them. Are they stubborn enough to hold out?"

Maxi nodded vigorously. "Missouri mules have nothing on those two."

While Glenn drove as fast as the road conditions allowed, I advised him where to turn. "There. That has to be the cottage. It has the kind of gray shutters Liza described."

Glenn stopped, stepped outside, and examined the tire marks in the driveway. "Someone has been here recently, but the wind blew some snow over the tracks."

I rushed to the nearest window and looked through the narrow slit where the drapes didn't quite meet. Maxi joined me. We looked through all the windows.

"We're too late," Glenn said. "There are tracks leading into the cottage and leading out."

Apparently thinking what I'd been thinking, Maxi muttered a few German words under her breath.

"I don't suppose you want to translate that?" Glenn asked with a grin.

"Some things don't translate," Maxi said, her tone lofty.

"Bringing the sisters to this isolated cottage makes sense, so why move them?" I wondered. "It's the perfect spot to do away with them."

"Something suddenly made the place unsafe," Glenn offered.

"Maybe that," I said, raising my chin toward the approaching snowplow.

The guy driving it stopped beside us. "You folks are early, ain't you? The Zimmerman reunion isn't until tomorrow."

"We just came to see how things are coming along," Maxi said.

"You'll get the road plowed by tomorrow?" I asked.

"Oh, yeah, if it takes till midnight." He raised a hand in greeting and resumed his task.

"Now we know why Francis had to move the sisters," Glenn said. "Tomorrow the place will be crawling with people. The question is where did he move them to?"

"Could Liza shed some light on that?" Maxi asked.

"She might. I know where she eats lunch. I'll join her."

Glenn used his cell phone. "Could I speak to Mr. Mac-Niall?" He waited. "No, there's no message." He slipped the phone into its case. "Francis is working at home this morning and isn't expected in until after lunch. I'll go back and stake out the mansion."

"I'll drive into town to meet Liza."

"And what's my assignment?" Maxi asked.

Looking at her hopeful expression, I couldn't just send her home. "Why don't you go to my office and answer the phone in case Rose calls. Or Jane Ann or Letty. I'll be there as soon as I've spoken to Liza."

* * *

I went to Joe's Eats where I was treated as if I were a regular. Joe brought me a pot of tea while I waited for Liza.

She came, lit a cigarette, and waved to Joe, who had her usual lunch ready.

"So, what's happening?" she asked, dousing her hot dog with mustard.

I told her that I suspected Francis of hiding the Washington sisters.

"Uncle Francis? I can't believe that. He's a cultured, sophisticated man. He wouldn't keep anyone against their will, much less kidnap them."

"He might when control of MacNiall Enterprises is at stake. Money and power are a strong motivation." I could tell she didn't want to believe this, but she was no longer completely certain about Uncle Francis. I watched her toy with the pickle on her plate.

I pressed on. "You think Francis would abdicate control of the family business to your mother without a fight?"

Liza sighed and shook her head. She pushed her plate away. "Why can't they go on as they are? Sharing the company? There's surely enough money and power to go around," she said, her voice bitter.

"Some people might be able to do that but do you think either one of them is good at sharing?"

"Mom certainly isn't, and Uncle Francis? I'm no longer sure what he's capable of," she admitted. "Still, I can't believe he'd take two old ladies and . . ." Her voice trailed off.

"Those two ladies know where your daughter is. Remember, Chelsea inherited a big chunk of company shares.

Whoever can get to her first and get her to vote their way will control vast wealth."

"So, my girl is a pawn to be used."

"Not if I find her first. Where could Francis have taken Letty and Jane Ann? Think, Liza."

Liza pressed her palms against her temples.

"He had them hidden in the hothouse, the third floor of the mansion, and then the cottage. What else does the family own where he could have hidden them?"

Liza stubbed out her cigarette and reached for a fresh one. I touched her hand to stop her. "You've barely touched your food."

"What are you? My mother?" Then she shook her head. "My mother never paid any attention to what I ate. Or if I ate. Only the nannies paid attention occasionally."

"If it's any consolation, my mother wasn't a model of maternal concern either, but luckily I had and still have a wonderful grandmother."

"I had the grandmother from Hades. All she cared about was that I used the correct fork and didn't spill anything at the dinner table." Liza paused, an aha-moment expression on her face. "Speaking of grandmothers, mine had a hunting lodge up in the woods."

"A hunting lodge?"

"The old biddy loved to shoot things."

"And your Uncle Francis knows where this lodge is?"

"Oh sure. He loves to shoot things too."

"Is it far from here?"

"About a four-hour drive north."

"Isolated?"

"Yeah. Deep in the woods. No neighbor for several miles."

"Could you draw a map of how to get there?"

"I doubt it. But I'll probably remember enough land-marks to get us there. We used to go up there a lot. Of course, it was a while ago."

"Still, it's worth a try. Can we get there this time of year?"

"Sure. It's a great area for snowmobilers, so they keep the roads plowed."

"Can you take off work this afternoon?"

"No, but I feel a bout of stomach flu coming on for to-morrow. Besides, leaving now wouldn't do us much good. By the time we got there, it would be dark. I know I can't find the lodge at night."

"Okay. We'll leave at six in the morning." I ignored her expression of dismay at the early hour and prayed that the sisters could survive the night. If they were up there. "I as-sume the place can be heated?"

Liza thought for a moment. "I remember a big fire-place in the main room."

Though Letty was on the scrawny side, she was muscu-lar enough to chop wood for the fireplace . . . if she wasn't tied up. But why should she be tied up, miles from any-where, without transportation, in snow-covered country? Surely Francis couldn't think that her sick sister could walk more than a few steps? If he took them. Or persuaded them to go away.

I paid our bill and drove to the agency.

"Hi, Oma. Any calls?" I asked Maxi, who sat behind my desk.

"Not a single call."

"Have you been bored?"

"No, though that's what Lynn thought, too, so she brought me some reports to type. I told her I wasn't familiar with the word processing program."

My mouth dropped open. "That woman has some nerve!"

Maxi smiled. "Don't worry. I got even. Had to call her up here several times to show me how to work the telephone, where you kept the tea kettle—"

"Oma, you're so bad." I had to smile back at her. I was sorry I had missed this battle of wills, which was only a minor version of the real fight: the battle over Uncle Barney. Both women loved him in their way and each distrusted the other.

"While I was sitting here, I accidentally looked at this yellow pad. What's with all the notations on county roads?"

"County roads?"

"You know, CR 70 and DR; CR 50 and MCR. All east-west roads in the county are numbered while the north-south ones have names."

Of course! How could I not have realized that the

abbreviations stood for locations? "DR is Davis Road but what is MCR?"

"McCracken Road. It's just south of my farm."

"So, you recognize all the locations?"

"Yes. You found the papers with the names on it in Shirley's house. Are they important?"

"They must be since they were hidden. I just don't know why. Yet." I glances at my watch. "There's enough time to look at them before it gets dark if we leave now."

Maxi followed me in her car. We parked at the first location and looked around.

"There's nothing here but soggy fields where the snow is melting," I said, regarding the intersection of CR 70 and Davis Road.

"In a few weeks soybeans or corn will be planted here," Maxi said.

"Let's look at the other places mentioned."

They all turned out to be fields. We stood and looked at the last location. "We must be missing something."

"Probably, but what? If we don't know what we're looking for, it's easy to miss something," Maxi pointed out.

"Okay, what do these locations have in common?"

"They're all fields."

"They're all corner lots at intersections of two roads."

"None of them are near a house."

"Hmm. The last two points might be significant," I said. "How so?"

"Being at an intersection makes them easy to find, and

not being near a house gives them a certain amount of privacy."

"So, if we wanted to do something here, we'd be unobserved, except for the occasional car driving by."

"Yes. The only question is what on earth would anybody want to do here?" Maxi looked as perplexed as I'm sure I did.

Even though the sun was shining and the temperature above the freezing point, it was still a little too cold to linger. "We're probably not asking the right questions," I said with a sigh. "Let's go home."

Promptly at six I rang Liza's doorbell. Moments later she came downstairs.

"Surprised that I'm ready?" she asked.

A little ashamed, I confessed that I was.

"Can we stop to get coffee? I'm not really awake until I have a cup."

"I went through the drive-thru and picked up two cups." I didn't like to drink coffee out of paper cups but we didn't have time for anything but a carryout.

We headed for the interstate and drove north for three-and-a-half hours before we turned west on a state road.

"Somewhere up ahead should be a little white church," Liza said. "Unless they painted it."

They hadn't.

"Keep going. In a while the road dead ends at a big field and we turn."

I kept driving slowly as the road was full of potholes.

Hitting one of those at high speed would not only get us a flat tire but probably dent the wheel as well.

When I reached the stop sign, I asked, "Do I turn right or left?"

"I don't remember all these houses here," she said.

"New housing developments go up all the time. You said it's been a while since you've been here."

"I think we always turned right."

I turned north and proceeded on a road that had even more potholes. At least it was daylight now and the sun had come out. Good. Maybe it would melt the rest of the snow.

Liza fidgeted. "Relax. If we're driving in the wrong direction, we'll turn around." We never got a chance to find out if we'd made the right choice. Up ahead a barricade barred the way. I stopped the car, and we got out.

"There's no way around the barricade." Just then I heard a car accelerate somewhere north of the barricade. I caught a brief glimpse of it. "Look straight ahead. Isn't that a car driving way from us?"

Liza shielded her eyes. "You're right. It's a car."

"A dark-colored big car?"

"It's too far away to be sure but yeah, I'd say it's a big, black sedan." She frowned. "How did it get around it?"

"I have no idea. Liza, how far is it to the lodge? Could we walk it?"

"Maybe, but it would take an hour or more."

"I wonder what the penalty is for removing a barricade?"

Whatever the penalty was seemed irrelevant as a county cop car drove up and stopped behind us. I watched a large man approach us. His hand was hooked on his belt, inches from the gun prominently resting against his pillarlike thigh.

"This road's closed, ladies."

"Why? It looks okay to me."

"Road work."

He wore dark glasses so I couldn't see his eyes, but if his voice was anything to go by, they wouldn't be friendly either.

"How long will it be closed?"

"Till next week."

"If the road's closed, how come I saw a sedan driving north just minutes ago?" I demanded.

"You're mistaken. There was no sedan."

"Yes, there was."

"Lady, I know my jurisdiction. There's been no traffic on this road. You saw nothing."

"Don't tell me what I saw or didn't see. My friend saw it too." I glanced at Liza who looked pale and scared. She shook her head ever so slightly.

"Maybe what we saw wasn't a car," she said, her voice small.

"Listen to your friend. Now get in your car and go back to where you came from. I'll watch to see that you leave okay and don't get stuck."

I wanted to tell him not to bother, but his hand was now firmly on the handle of his gun. I hated to admit it, but it was prudent to leave.

I backed up, careful not to scrape his bumper though I

badly wanted to floor the accelerator and smash right into his car. I drove, my teeth clenched so hard my jaw began to ache.

"I'm sorry I couldn't back you up, but he's the kind of cop who'd have loved nothing better than to run us in if we'd given him the slightest excuse. I've met his kind before."

She was probably right. My opinion of cops was colored by my cousin, Sam, who was one of the good ones.

"Liza, in the glove compartment there's a notebook and a pen. Take them out. Then use the vanity mirror to get his license plate. Be careful he doesn't see what you're doing."

"No problem. He'll think I'm primping."

He tapped his horn and waved us on.

"Don't you just love being ordered around by a guy whose shoe size is probably bigger than his IQ?" she asked.

"Love it."

"What gives him the right to order us around like that?"

"That gun on his hip."

"Is he following us?"

"Yes." He did until we reached the state road and turned east. He turned west, and I breathed easier.

"Now what?" Liza asked.

"I'm driving back to that service station, and then I'm phoning Uncle Barney for instructions. And later I'm driving right through that barricade."

Chapter Eleven

Unfortunately Lynn was the only person in the office. I informed her of my location and that I was going to walk to the MacNiall hunting lodge. I told her to check in with Liza who was staying at the service station. As soon as I finished the call, Liza protested.

"Wouldn't it be wise to have someone whose last name is MacNiall with you when you get to the lodge?"

I hated to admit it, but she had a point. Still, if I ran into trouble, I'd prefer to do it alone. It wouldn't look good if the agency endangered the daughter of a client.

"I need you to be our liaison. You have the office number and Glenn's cell, right?"

Liza nodded. "Promise to phone every half hour."

"If I can." Liza didn't like this, but there was nothing she could do about that.

I turned the car around, and we switched seats. She drove me back to the barricade and watched me climb over it. I motioned for her to turn around and drive back to the service station and waited until she did. Only then did I set off toward the hunting lodge.

I started out jogging, but soon slowed to a brisk walk as I had no idea what I would encounter at the lodge. Whatever it might be, it was better if I didn't arrive all out of breath and exhausted. True to my word, I phoned Liza.

"Where are you?" she asked.

"Hunkered down in the road. I can see the lodge. That sedan we saw is parked in front. I'm going to have to circle around and sneak up on the house."

"I still think I should have come with you. Call me as soon as you've peeked through the window. Cybil, if I don't hear from you in the next twenty minutes, I'll ram that barricade and drive straight up to the lodge."

"Okay, okay. Don't do anything rash. I've got to go."

Sneaking up on the house was harder than I thought it would be. For one thing, in front of the lodge there was no cover, nothing to hide behind, which meant I had to crawl far enough to the left so I couldn't be seen from the house. By the time I reached the lodge, I was perspiring. It was time to phone Liza before she rammed the barricade.

"Hey, I'm outside the lodge," I whispered.

"What are you going to do?" Liza asked.

"I haven't figured that out exactly, but I surely would like to know what's being said inside." Ducking down, I worked my way to the window. I crouched underneath it and strained to listen. Though I could hear the murmur of voices, I couldn't make out the words.

"Be careful," Liza whispered.

Before I could say say anything, two sharp popping sounds made me jump, hitting the top of my head on the bottom of the window frame.

"What was—"

A third shot caused me to throw myself flat onto the snow.

"Are those gunshots?" Liza asked, her voice terrified.

"Yes." Glenn had insisted on giving me shooting lessons, so I was acquainted with the sound of a handgun.

"Who's shooting at you?"

"Nobody. It's happening in the cabin. I'll call you back." I called 911, reported tersely that I'd heard shots and gave them the location. I dropped the phone into my pocket and sprinted to the door. I pressed myself against the wall right next to it before I spoke. "Jane Ann? Letty? Are you in there? Are you okay? This is Cybil Quindt. I'm—"

I was interrupted by a high-pitched scream. Letty's voice, I thought. I edged to the window and took a couple of deep breaths before I risked a quick look inside. I saw Jane Ann clinging to the door of the back room which I assumed was a bedroom. I couldn't see Letty, but judging from the sound of her voice, she had to be near the front entrance. I couldn't see where the person belonging to the sedan was.

Dashing back to the door, I shouted, "I called nine-one-one! Help should be here soon."

I waited but there was no reply. Hearing some movements, I said, "Letty, I'm coming in."

"Wait a minute," she called back.

I did. Then I turned the knob. The door opened.

Letty stood in the middle of the room, a pistol in her hand. As I stepped inside, I almost tripped over something on the floor. It took a fraction of a second before I realized that the something was a body. The body of a man.

I bent down and felt the side of his neck for a pulse. There was one, though it was weak. "This man has been shot," I said unnecessarily, watching the puddle of blood spread around him.

"He shot at me first," Letty said. "I shot back in self-defense."

I took off my scarf and held it out to her. "Put your gun on this scarf." When she hesitated, I said, my voice hard, "Now!" I was hoping that putting the gun into the scarf wouldn't mess up the fingerprints, but even more importantly, I needed to get it away from her before she decided to shoot someone else. Me maybe.

Reluctantly, she placed the gun on the scarf, which I put on the floor behind me.

"Now get some clean towels before this man bleeds to death."

She did. I pressed them against his side and his arm where blood was seeping through his coat. Only then did I see his face. Startled, I looked at Letty. "You shot Francis MacNiall."

"He shot at me first," she said in the petulant tone of a child invoking the tit-for-tat law.

Her lower lip quivered, and she started to weep noisily.

I thought the crying sounded phony. Feeling my phone vibrate, I answered it.

"What's happening?" Liza asked.

"I'm in the cabin. Letty Washington shot your Uncle Francis. He's alive but bleeding badly."

"I'm coming in."

"The ambulance will get here hopefully before you do."

"Maybe not. I didn't go back to the service station. I'm at the barricade which I'm dismantling as we speak. I'll be at the cabin in a jiffy."

Since it was Liza's uncle who'd been shot, I didn't try to stop her.

The ambulance, two squad cars, and Liza arrived in that order.

The EMTs worked swiftly and allowed Liza to ride to the hospital with them. As soon as they left, silence descended onto the room. Jane Ann and Letty sat stiffly side by side on the sofa, the sheriff in the rocking chair, and I perched on a footstool. Nobody said anything. The only sound was that made by the rocking chair. The sheriff looked peaceful and relaxed, but I wasn't taken in by his easy pose, not when the corners of his mouth were turned down and his eyes cold and suspicious. And not when a pile of bloody towels lay on the floor, mute testimony of what had happened.

"Mrs. Quindt, why don't you tell me again why you're here and what you observed," the sheriff said.

I had already told him twice. Knowing that he was trying to trip me up or trick me into revealing something new, I repeated my story as verbatim as I could. I could tell he didn't like that. Silently I congratulated myself but promised myself not to tell it again. Before the ambulance had left, I'd managed to phone Uncle Barney and told him what had happened. He advised minimal disclosure of the facts and nothing more.

"So, you claim you're trying to find your client's granddaughter."

"Yes, Sheriff."

"And you claim that these two ladies know where she is."

"They know the name of the couple to whom they sold the baby."

"No, we don't. That was seventeen years ago. We're elderly and our memories aren't what they used to be," Letty said with a self-pitying expression on her long, thin face.

"Yeah, right." I didn't bother to camouflage the sarcasm in my voice.

"And we didn't sell the baby. We merely accepted a fee for our services."

"Sell. Charge a fee. Semantics. You had no right to do anything with that baby. Her mother never agreed to give her away," I said.

"She was a seventeen-year-old kid. A minor. Her mother

and her grandmother had every right to take charge," Letty claimed.

"Ladies! That's for the courts to decide. Our immediate concern is the shooting. You heard the shots?"

"Yes," I answered.

"Miss Washington, were you in the room when the shots were fired?" he asked Jane Ann.

"No. I was on my way to the living room, but I can only move slowly, so I didn't see the actual shooting."

"How many shots did you hear?" he asked.

"Three."

"And you, Miss Letty?"

"I told you. Mr. MacNiall shot at me and I shot back. It was self-defense."

"You shot him twice?"

"Yes."

"Where did you get the gun?"

"It was our daddy's. He left it to me, and he taught me how to shoot. I have a permit."

"Are you a good shot?"

"Yes."

"So why did you have to shoot him twice?"

"I wasn't sure I'd hit him the first time."

"Even though you are a good shot?"

The sheriff was skeptical and so was I. Something kept nagging at me, but with all that had happened, I couldn't think straight. The smell of blood was thick in the small room, making me feel dizzy and nauseated.

"Sheriff, may I go outside? The smell—"

"Sorry, but not yet. Not until the crime-scene team gets here." He glanced at his watch. "Should be any minute now."

He walked around, checking the walls of the cabin, looking for a bullet hole, I presumed. "May I open the door?"

"Just a crack. It's cold in here."

I opened the door and stuck my head out. The air was cold and bracing and smelled clean. I took deep breaths until a couple of vans pulled up. I was allowed to stay by the open door, but the sisters had to wait in the back room while the technicians did their thing.

The sheriff joined me.

"Will they test Mr. MacNiall's hands to see if he fired a gun?" I asked.

"At the hospital? Doubtful. Unless I request it. Why, do you think it's necessary?"

"Wasn't the pistol a little far from his hand? The pistol he supposedly fired at Letty?"

The sheriff glanced at the chalk outlines on the floor. "Maybe, maybe not. What else is bothering you about this shooting? You know these people. I don't."

I stepped outside and looked at the spot under the window. "You can see my footprints. I was crouched there when I heard the first two shots. They startled me so much that I jumped up and bumped my head on the window frame. When I heard the third shot, I threw myself on the ground. Two—"

"There were three shots."

"Yes, but the sequence doesn't jibe with Letty's version. Two shots were close together, one right after the other. The third shot was a second or two later."

The sheriff rubbed his chin, thinking for a moment. "He didn't shoot first."

"No, he didn't. He might not have fired a pistol at all. I pressed towels against his right side and against his right arm. With wounds like that, could he have picked up a gun? I've met him before, and I'm pretty sure he's right handed."

"I'll speak to the physician treating him. If his answer is no, that skinny woman in there might not have shot in self-defense." He paused and gave me a sideways look. "Any idea why she'd shoot him?"

"An old story that involves power and money."

"Doesn't it always?" he asked and shook his head.

"What will you do with the sisters?"

"Take them to the office to make a statement."

"Before you do, could I speak to Jane Ann? She's the invalid. It has nothing to do with the shooting."

"Make it brief."

A deputy, his hand firmly on Letty's arm, led her to the squad car. When the second deputy brought Jane Ann from the back, the sheriff motioned him to stop.

"Jane Ann—"

"Cybil, tell Maxi what's happening. We need help. The church has an attorney. He'll probably know the name of a lawyer up here who can help us."

"I'll do that, but I need a favor from you. The name of the couple who adopted Chelsea."

"I honestly don't know the name but the mother was a pharmacist. In a town the size of ours, how many fiftysomething lady pharmacists can there be?"

"Thanks, Jane Ann. I'll call Maxi."

After the squad cars drove off, I did. Naturally I had to tell my grandmother everything that had happened before I drove home.

Maxi was already parked in front of my house when I got there. I had to assure her repeatedly that I was fine.

When she was satisfied that I was okay, she asked if I was hungry.

"Now that you mention it, I'm starved. I had toast and coffee this morning and nothing since then."

"Good. I brought food. Enough to feed Luke too."

A car I recognized as belonging to my husband parked in front of my house. We waited for Luke to carry Maxi's basket of food into the kitchen for her. Then he came back into the hall to hang up his coat.

My little orange tabby cat came and rubbed herself against Luke's legs. Me she ignored.

"Buddy, you little ingrate. Don't come later and beg to sleep on my bed," I told her.

"Can I come and beg to sleep on your bed?" Luke asked in a low voice.

"In your dreams."

His grin was wickedly sexy. "In my dreams I do that all the time."

I was saved from trying to find an appropriate remark by Maxi's voice, summoning us to eat. I scrubbed my hands again, though I had already done so twice. I kept imagining blood on them.

"Stuffed green peppers," Luke exclaimed. "Haven't had any of those since last summer."

"Krogers had these beauties. Imported from South America," Maxi said, pleased by Luke's enthusiastic response.

Even though I had been hungry, I had trouble getting food down my throat. I prayed Maxi wouldn't notice, but she did.

"Schatzi, you are not okay."

I could feel Luke's attention shift to me.

"What happened?" he demanded.

"Cybil found another body," she said and patted my arm.

"Not a body," I protested. "He was alive. The EMTs thought he'd make it." My voice sounded the way it did just before the tears came. I willed myself not to cry. "He was shot in the right side and the right arm. Wounds there aren't fatal, are they?" I pleaded for Luke to reassure me, but being conscientious, he wouldn't lie to me.

"Survival depends on several things. Tell me everything."

I did.

He listened attentively. "If the man was in good health, he should survive these injuries."

"I don't know anything about his health, but he's not a young man."

"So, if Francis MacNiall dies, Letty will face murder charges unless she can convince the police and the DA that it was self-defense," Maxi said. "There was always something sneaky about her, but I never thought her capable of shooting someone in cold blood."

"I don't think this was done in cold blood. She might have been frightened into shooting him. He probably threatened her again."

"Again?" Luke asked.

"The phony repairman who started the fire in their house. I'm now convinced it was Francis."

"I think you're right," Maxi said, "but proving that will be next to impossible."

"And his reason for doing all this?" Luke asked, his expression skeptical.

"The family business. A multimillion dollar enterprise," I said.

"Whoever can get control of Chelsea's shares controls the company," Maxi added. "And the Washington sisters may know who adopted her."

"You still haven't found the girl? What happens if you don't?" Luke asked.

"Rose and Francis go on administering together. Or until one can persuade some stockholders to sell him or her their shares."

"That could get messy," he said.

"Very." Suddenly I remembered Jane Ann's tip. "Luke,

do you know any fiftysomething women pharmacists in Westport?"

"I know two. Both work in the hospital pharmacy."

"Do they have children? Daughters? One who is seventeen and adopted?"

"Chelsea?" Maxi asked, leaning forward with great interest.

I told her what Jane Ann had said.

"The adoptive parents could have moved away. Seventeen years is a long time," Luke said.

We were all thinking quietly. Then something occurred to me. "Luke, don't pharmacists have professional associations?"

"I'm sure they do. Why?"

"I have to call Uncle Barney," I said and hurried to the phone. He was at home and agreed that this was a lead worth pursuing. He'd get Glenn to start a computer search.

When I came into the kitchen, I was too restless to sit. I paced the floor.

The phone rang. I let the machine pick it up. It was the automated sub finder of the school corporation, asking if I wanted to sub the next day.

That's when it hit me. "Yes! That's what has been nagging at me. Annette Ferris."

"Who's Annette Ferris?" Luke asked.

"A teacher I've been volunteering for." I grabbed my purse and rummaged through it. "I have her number here somewhere."

"I didn't know you were that eager to volunteer," Maxi said, a bit bewildered.

"I'm not, but Annette has a seventeen-year-old adopted sister."

"She's probably not the only adopted seventeen-year-old," Luke pointed out in his maddeningly logical manner.

"No, but how many have mothers who are pharmacists?"

"Oh, my!" Maxi exclaimed.

Luke took the purse from my hand and dumped its contents on the table. "Knowing that you have everything in here except the proverbial kitchen sink, isn't this easier?"

"Yes, smarty. Thank you." I found the card but discovered that my hands shook. Luke dialed the number for me.

"Annette, this is Cybil Quindt. Hi. May I ask you a question?"

"Sure."

"Did you not tell me that you had an adopted sister who's seventeen and that your mom is a pharmacist?"

"Yes to both questions."

"And her nickname is Ceecee which stands for?"

"Cynthia Chelsea. Cynthia for my grandmother and Chelsea is the name her biological mother gave her."

"I'm going to have to sit down," I murmured and did. Luke looked at me curiously and Maxi made those curled finger motions with both hands that demanded more information. "Does Ceecee have a birthmark?" I held my breath.

"Why, yes. How did you know?"

"Where is it?"

"On the inside of her upper left arm. Why?"

I expelled the breath I'd been holding. "Has Ceecee ever expressed an interest in finding her biological mother?"

"Ever since she turned fourteen, but my parents didn't think it was possible because the adoption wasn't arranged through regular channels. I suspect they were also afraid that Ceecee might be taken away from them, so they begged her to wait until she turned eighteen."

Annette paused, and I prepared myself for her next question.

"Do you know who her mother is?"

"Yes."

"Did she hire you to find Ceecee?"

"Her grandmother did."

"What happens next?" Annette asked.

"I'm not sure, but we have to inform our client that we found her granddaughter."

I phoned Uncle Barney who took over at this point.

I hadn't forgotten my promise to Liza. It took me a while to figure out a way to tip her off without violating the agency's confidentiality clause.

When she came back to town after Francis was released from the hospital, I met her in front of Joe's Eats.

"Can't stay away from the place?" she asked with a smile.

"Who could resist its ambiance?" Then I grew serious. "I have to talk to you about something."

She took a deep breath. "You've found Chelsea."

"You know I can't tell you anything, but if I were you, I'd visit your mother. Watch her. Follow her to see whom she meets. Just a suggestion."

Liza threw her arms around me. "Thank you, thank you."

"I didn't tell you anything, and you're welcome." I saw tears in her eyes.

"How will I know her?"

Remembering the family portrait on Annette's desk at school, I said, "Take a look at a picture of yourself when you were seventeen." I gave her a quick hug. "I have to go. "Remember, she'll turn eighteen in a few months and can decide where and with whom she wants to live." I turned and walked away quickly.

"Thank you again. And bless you," she called after me.

I raised my hand in a wave but kept walking. I had to because tears filled my eyes. I blinked them away. It wouldn't do for an apprentice PI to become maudlin.

Chapter Twelve

In the days that followed, I felt restless and unsettled. The weather had turned warmer. By the middle of March, the last of the snow had melted. Everything was soggy and messy.

I had written my reports and turned them in to Uncle Barney, who told me I had done a good job and took me to lunch. Now I was sitting at my desk with nothing but routine filing to do, which I loathed. Still, I was getting paid so I had to do something. I took everything out of my in-tray and organized it into stacks.

One stack contained my notes on the MacNiall case. Though the state of Michigan would decide what to do about the shooting at the lodge which was in its jurisdiction, as far as the agency was concerned the case was closed. Still, I wasn't completely satisfied. Maybe because the murders of Shirley and Rodney were still open cases and the trail was getting cold. The crime scene people hadn't been able to match the third blood type found in the living room. Maybe I couldn't let go of the case because I didn't know who'd locked me into that shed. Maybe because in unguarded moments the bloody carnage in the Dwyer home still flashed through my mind and frequently invaded my dreams. I wanted—needed—closure.

According to his sister-in-law, Francis MacNiall was recovering nicely at home. His attorney had issued one of those generic statements that said nothing. Francis claimed he couldn't remember what happened in the lodge. I'd pestered Sam until he phoned his colleagues in Michigan to inquire about the case. They'd tested the guns and found that both had been fired in the lodge that day. Tests revealed that both Letty and Francis had fired a gun, but since both had lawyered up and refused to speak, we might never know who fired first.

Rose MacNiall had come in person to pay her bill and to thank us for finding Chelsea. She had met her granddaughter whom she pronounced to be smart and sweet, though a tad independent. Silently I applauded the girl for that and hoped that this independent streak would keep her from becoming a pawn in the family power struggle.

Liza phoned to tell me that she had contrived to meet her daughter and that she would do everything in her power to protect her from her new family. I told her I wished her luck and hoped she would succeed. Before she hung up, I asked the question that had been nagging me.

"Liza, did you ask your mother what happened to your other baby?"

"Yes. She admitted that I'd given birth to twins but that one of the babies didn't make it. For once I believe her. You'll never guess where her little grave is."

I had one of those moments of blinding insights. "The stone angel in the garden."

Liza gasped. "How did you know?"

"Just an inspired guess."

"You'll be pleased to know that I've stopped smoking, which is killing me. I also no longer eat or drink lunch at Dirty Joe's. I want to set a good example for Chelsea."

"That's great. Keep in touch."

She promised she would.

That left the Washington sisters. Maxi had helped them obtain legal representation but had heard nothing further from them. I suspected that there would be some heavy plea bargaining going on to avoid a trial involving three senior citizens, one of whom was ill, one recovering from gunshot wounds, and one a nervous wreck.

With a sigh I studied the first stack. On top was the copy of the note I'd found hidden in Shirley Dwyer's house. CR 70 & DR. What could that mean? There was nothing at that intersection. Maybe there was and I had missed it. Now that the snow had melted, perhaps I could find something. Besides, a trip into the country was more appealing than filing reports. And I could stop to say hello to my grandmother.

I made a quick decision, grabbed my purse and coat,

and drove to Maxi's farm. She was eager to get out of the house and volunteered to go with me.

I parked at the intersection of CR 70 and DR. We both got out of the car and looked around. What we saw was a county road and a side road full of potholes.

"There's nothing here that shouldn't be here. Is there?" I asked.

"Nothing that is obviously out of place," Maxi agreed. She walked closer to the ditch and, holding onto the sign post, she peered down into it. "Cybil, your eyes are better than mine, but doesn't it look like that patch of dirt has sunk lower than the rest?"

I looked. "Yes, it does. What would cause it to sink down like that?"

"If someone had dug up the soil relatively recently and had buried something, the soil would eventually settle and look a bit sunken in."

We looked at each other. "There's only one way to find out." I got the shovel I kept in the trunk of my car in case I got stuck in the snow and began to dig. The wet earth was heavy. After a few minutes I took off my coat and handed it to Maxi.

"You have another shovel in your car?" she asked.

"No." Even if I had, there was no way I'd let my grandmother dig. About two feet down, my shovel hit something hard. "Must be a big rock," I said, slightly out of breath. I dug to the left of it and to the right but kept hitting something solid. "No rock is that big," I said. I lifted the soil out of the way and saw something metallic.

"Cybil, dig carefully. We don't want to destroy or damage what's down there."

"I'll treat this like an archaeological dig. Not that I've been on one, but I often watch the History Channel and they're always showing digs." About fifteen minutes later, I saw what I'd unearthed and scrambled hastily out of the ditch.

"What is it?" Maxi asked.

"A barrel marked Hazardous Waste."

"*Maria und Josef*!" Maxi exclaimed.

This was as close as Maxi came to blaspheming. She was that shocked.

"Who would be so careless, so stupid, so irresponsible as to bury dangerous materials two feet down on farm land?" she wondered out loud.

"I suspect Rodney Dwyer was. Or at least he knew who buried it."

"But where did he get the dangerous material?" Maxi asked.

I thought for a moment. "Who has the largest factory in a tri-county area, protected by a high fence and security guards?"

"The MacNialls."

I nodded. "I suspect burying this stuff is what got Rodney and his mother killed."

"I can't imagine Rose MacNiall condoning this."

"She might not have known about this."

"How many more places were mentioned on that paper?"

"Two more, but that doesn't mean that there aren't more. Or that there aren't others buried in this ditch. It's miles long. Let's check out the two we know about."

At CR 50 and MCR we found another barrel of hazardous waste. At the last site my spade struck a different object. Maxi and I stared at each other in disbelief when I brushed off the soil from the first one I dug up.

"Now we know what they did with all those Mason jars," Maxi said.

"And what they did with the money Rodney received for burying the hazardous waste."

"Rather ingenious, stuffing the cash into glass jars and burying them. I'll never look at canning jars the same way," Maxi said.

That was too bad, I thought selfishly, for I loved Maxi's canned peaches. "Time to call the sheriff. By now he's probably sick to death of hearing from me."

He was, judging by the long-suffering look he flashed me when he joined us. After the OSHA people arrived to supervise the safe removal of the waste materials, he told us we could leave. I hesitated.

"What?" Maxi asked.

I turned to the lawman. "Sheriff, the person who is responsible for dumping this isn't going to get away with it, is he?"

His face turned brick red. "Why would you even ask me that?"

I shrugged elaborately.

"This time he's messed with a federal agency, so payoffs

to local officials aren't going to sweep this mess under the rug."

He almost smiled.

Maxi's elbow poked me in my side. "Federal?"

"OSHA is part of the Department of Labor."

"Oh."

"Look," I pointed to a van that sported the logo of our newspaper on its side. "The Fourth Estate has arrived. I doubt that this story is going to be buried on the back page."

It wasn't. Next morning a picture of one of the barrels formed the center piece on the front page.

Predictably, the MacNialls refused to comment beyond a released statement that claimed they always subcontracted the removal of the waste to several supposedly reputable companies. They were, therefore, not responsible.

"Not responsible?" I yelled, causing Buddy to stop eating her breakfast and stare at me. Her fluffy tail thumped the floor.

There's no proof of any wrongdoing, the spokesperson claimed.

I threw the empty corn flakes box across the room. No proof. The words taunted me.

"We'll see about that." I had to make one more trip to Shirley's house. Somewhere in there had to be proof linking the MacNialls to the illegal dumping. If the sheriff caught me, so be it. Besides, I couldn't imagine him not being upset by the MacNialls's abdication of responsibility.

Half an hour later I let myself into the Dwyer home. Fleetingly I recalled Uncle Barney's orders that I wasn't to come here alone. As a sop to my conscience, I left a message of my whereabouts on Glenn's machine.

The house was cold and quiet, yet didn't feel empty, as if the spirits of its owners were still lingering. I felt compelled to address them in a low voice.

"Sorry, Shirley and Rodney, for disturbing you and invading your privacy again, but I need one piece of evidence in the toxic waste scandal. Or one on who murdered you, though the orders for both probably came from the same source."

If I'd been more superstitious, I'd have pleaded for help from otherworldly sources. Since I wasn't, I set out to do a deep, systematic search. Since my previous search of the kitchen had been the most thorough, I started at the front of the house.

This might be my last chance to look around, as the estate was being settled and the house sold. I stood in the middle of Shirley's bedroom. The Dwyers had had a penchant for burying things, for stuffing them into hollowed out objects that were not unlike coffins. Jeez, now I was growing fanciful. Still . . .

I picked up a music box, the kind given as a prize at a county fair's shooting booth. Curious as to what tune it played, I looked for the key to wind it up. I couldn't find it. I shook the box and heard a faint noise. I needed a sharp object to open it. My gaze fell on Shirley's sewing box. A good-sized plastic cube, it had a tray for spools of thread, packets of needles, tape measures, and objects I had no idea what they were used for. And scissors, the perfect tool for my needs.

What I found was part of a photo, showing the legs of a man standing at the edge . . . of a ditch? The dark slacks and the bottom of the dark winter coat in the picture could belong to anyone, but the shoes were another matter. I had come across mention of shoes like that before. Now all I had to do was find the other three parts of the photo.

It took the better part of an hour before I found the rest, encased in a plastic sandwich bag in the bottom of a shoe box. I had almost replaced the lid without lifting the sneakers out because they were dirty, smelly, and disreputable looking. Few would be tempted to pick them up. "Clever, Rodney, clever," I murmured.

I sat down on the floor to think. Then I phoned the sheriff.

"I know who killed the Dwyers, and I think we can prove it," I said without preamble.

"Yeah? Who and how?"

He sounded skeptical, and I couldn't blame him. "You still have the blood of the unknown third person from the living room?"

"Of course. It's in the medical examiner's lab."

"If you can get the technicians to compare it to the blood the crime scene people took from the floor next to Francis MacNiall in that lodge, you'll find that it's identical." I thought I heard a noise outside like a car passing, but I was so caught up in trying to convince the sheriff that I ignored it.

"You're wondering about the motive," I rushed on. "It's that illegally dumped hazardous waste. Rodney was blackmailing Francis. Maybe even threatening to expose him."

"Interesting. Your proof?"

"A photo showing Francis standing at the intersection of County Road 70 and Davis Road, watching two men lower a barrel of toxic waste into the ditch."

"You're sure it's him?"

"Yes. Whoever took the photo—and I suspect it was Rodney—made darn sure that it was in focus. It's as if he were holding a smoking gun. We got him." I knew I sounded triumphant but I couldn't help myself.

"Where are you?"

"At the Dwyer house."

"Alone?"

"Yes."

"I don't like that."

I heard him order the unit closest to the Dwyer house to proceed there.

"I'm on my way," he said and hung up.

His concern creeped me out a bit. It intensified when a big car pulled into the driveway and stopped behind my car. I watched from a safe distance behind the lace curtain, certain that in the dark house I couldn't be seen from outside. I stuck the baggy inside my tights where it rested securely just above my knee. When the car door opened and

I saw who the driver was, adrenaline flooded my body. I gasped when I saw the gun he was holding against his leg.

Had he been watching the house? Had he followed me? Had he come to search for the incriminating evidence once more? It didn't matter why he had come. By now he knew what kind of car I drove, and he knew I was in the house.

I dropped to the floor and duck walked as fast as I could toward the kitchen. As I passed the pantry, I saw that the window was cracked open. I eased it up just wide enough to hoist myself through and drop to the ground. I hesitated a moment, wondering which way to run. Could I outrun a bullet? Hardly. Not unless I got enough of a head start. Could I stay hidden until the sheriff or one of his deputies arrived? That was too much like being a sitting duck and far too frightening. Better to do something.

I crawled toward the front of the house, keeping close to its wall. The ground was cold and damp. I heard him move through the house. He knew I was here as I had foolishly left my car in the driveway. The way he had parked, he'd boxed me in. I knew I could outrun him but not his fancy, powerful car.

Disable the car. It was as if a voice had whispered this into my ear. Disable how? In the movies the villain removed something from under the hood—a distributor? A distributor cap? Even if I had known what that part looked like and if I could pop the hood, I didn't think my nemesis would stand by idly and let me do this. But if I managed to sneak unseen to his car, I could do something to his tires.

Uncle Barney had given me a Swiss Army knife for my birthday and made me promise to carry it always in my purse. I took it out and examined it. In addition to the blade it had several interesting attachments. The question was whether any of them were strong enough to puncture a tire. Maybe the corkscrew. No time like the present to find out.

I heard him move to the back of the house where he would discover the partially open window. It was sticking badly and trying to close it would have wasted precious minutes. Taking a deep breath for strength and courage, I sprinted to his car. I hunkered down by the back wheel on the driver's side and jabbed the corkscrew several times into the tire. For good measure I stabbed it with the blade. Then I took off running in the direction of the highway where there was lots of traffic. Surely he wouldn't shoot me in front of witnesses.

Though I couldn't hear anything above my labored breathing and the hard beating of my heart, the hair on the back of my neck bristled. I risked a quick look over my shoulder and promptly stumbled. Recovering, I increased my speed, for coming up fast behind me was MacNiall's big, black killing machine, aimed straight at me. Drat. My attack on his tire hadn't been successful. Scratch a career as a saboteur.

Glancing at both sides of the road, I saw a line of trees on the right, demarcating the boundary line between two farms. My salvation, if I could reach it before the car hit me. I scrambled across the deep ditch, and separating the two bottom strands of barbed wire, I crawled through them. One of my gloves and the back of my jacket got caught in the fence. Struggling to free them, I heard the familiar popping sound. Francis was shooting at me. I slipped my hand out of my glove and my arms out of my jacket, leaving both of them hostages to the fence. I felt a hot sting on my arm. Apparently I hadn't escaped the sharp prongs of the wire. Ignoring the pain, I zigzagged toward the trees.

My goal was a majestic oak. It was nearest and its trunk was reassuringly broad and thick. I collapsed behind it. After my breathing slowed a little, I risked a look backward. I saw revolving flashes of light. Patrol cars. Then there was Glenn, looking at my abandoned coat.

He cupped his hands around his mouth and called my name. I stood and waved. Then I started toward him, cradling my right arm, which now hurt considerably.

"Did you get Francis MacNiall? He shot at me," I said when we met.

"Yeah, we got him."

Glenn took one look at my arm, whipped out his cell, and called for an ambulance.

"It's just sort of a scratch," I protested. "I tangled with the barbed wire. If you call an ambulance, it'll take me to the emergency room and Luke will never let me hear the end of this."

"If I don't, *I'll* never hear the end of it. You think I want to face Barney? Maxi? Not on your life."

Glenn deftly wrapped his scarf around my upper arm.

"Turn around," I said.

"Why?"

"So I can get the incriminating photo out of my tights."

"Oh." Glenn turned away.

"I've got to give this to the sheriff." I took the photo out of the baggy and showed it to Glenn.

He whistled. "That should cook his goose but good."

I must have swayed, for Glenn grabbed my left arm.

"Can you walk down to the road?" he asked.

"Of course. I didn't hurt my legs." Despite my brave words I felt a little woozy. The distance to the road seemed suddenly very far. I'm not sure I would have made it without Glenn's steadying arm around my shoulder.

I remember leaning against Glenn's car, feeling so tired I wanted to slide to the ground. Then the next thing I knew I was being lifted out of the ambulance and wheeled into an examination room. Luke's handsome face loomed over me.

"That's another fine mess you got yourself into," he said.

"Your imitation of Laurel and Hardy could use some work." I managed a weak smile. "What's happening?"

"You got shot," Luke said. "Fortunately the bullet missed the bone in your arm. We'll fix you up good as new, but you'll have to keep your arm in a sling for the next five years."

"Five—"

"No chasing of murderers, embezzlers, blackmailers, and other assorted criminals."

"You wish."

"I do."

Luke bent down and kissed me gently. Just then I didn't care if I ever chased another criminal.